Crabquake!

SJ Stone

Published by SJ Stone, 2023.

To Mike: We miss you!

To Mike: We miss you!

Acknowledgments

Crabquake was born of two things – my love of National Novel Writing Money and the idea that Sharknado was such a garbage movie that I should be able to write something just as bad. And so, in the vein of the latter and via the vehicle of the former, Crabquake was born.

When did this happen? I feel like it was seven years ago, but Covid screwed up how everyone perceives time, so I can't be sure. Regardless, I wrote the book during NaNo in approximately 30 days, and it came in around 62k words, which is just a little longer than Stephen King's famous horror novel Carrie.

During the years leading up to this publishing, I spent a lot of time on other writing projects. That, it seems, is the writer's life. Write everything, sometimes 2-3 WIPs at the same time, maybe finish one, then just keep going on to the next and the next. The thrill of writing is in the discovery of the story, not the editing, rewrites, and publishing. Those are the grueling parts of writing. That's where all the work happens. So, it's easy to finish a project, declare victory and go on to the next. And I did. Only now, ten or more years after I've written 3-4 novels, and even finished a few, I've decided to do the grown-up work of the novelist – edit, rewrite and polish for publication. Create the social media bits. Make a website. Write a blurb, a premise, some literature for the front and back of the book, even an author bio. Blech!

Where's the fun in that, you may ask? I'm not sure, but I do know that if you don't do that, no one else is ever going to get to read your book. So, here we are. And now I'm sitting back thinking about Haze and Jesse and their adventure and hoping that you'll have as much fun with it as I did. I hope that if you live in Baltimore, or did, that you can picture exactly where my characters are, what they see, the places they visit. I was very purposeful in my choice of location for several reasons, and as I pointed out to someone today on Twitter, the plot of the book goes right by my old house to a park where my kids used to play. I even destroyed a restaurant that we loved to go to when a dear friend owned it. And for that reason, Mike, I will dedicate this novel to you. Because we loved you and your place, and now that you've passed away and we don't really go to your old place anymore, I'm just going to let Crabquake wreck it and leave us with one more fond memory.

And to my wife, who is a cut-throat editor – not a pro, but not afraid to tell me what she thinks, I thank you. It pains me sometimes to sit up here and click away on my keyboard and leave you sitting downstairs with the dogs at night, so thanks for being so understanding and letting me deal with all the characters that are clamoring for attention inside my head. And thanks for helping steer them down their paths when you're editing.

And that is that. What comes next is a silly adventure novel I've told the SyFy Channel on Twitter more than once would be an excellent shitty movie on their channel (like all their movies). I hope you enjoy it!

-SJ Stone

1

"WHAT THE FUCK WE DOING out here, D? Streetlights still on."

"Keep it down, yo. We creepin'."

"Creepin' on what, dog? You drug my ass out here. We applying for jobs? I got a fucking job."

"No, not jobs, but we on a job. And don't even tell me 'bout your job, slave ass nigga working for the white man."

"Fuck you, D, I ain't working for the white man. Told you the dude is Chinese anyway, and the shit pays good. Lots of paper in Canton, and I'm getting some so I can hit that culinary art school and move on up. Move the fuck out. Ain't doing West Side no more. You and your "slave" bullshit coming at me first thing - sun ain't even up, dog, and I was there till almost three. Now I'm out here with your ass in the dark, this damn fog, doing whatever this bullshit is. I got a job, D."

"Uh huh. Slopping arts and cheeses and white wines to uppity ass white bitches and their white masters in their tight high-end rides. Franklin Douglas woulda turned over in his grave over that shit. You betraying the heritage, yo. His building right over there and all." He nodded without looking at the angular black structure that marked the west end of Fells Point.

"It's Fredrick Douglas, you ignorant muthafucka. If you want to quote shit from history, you might wanna get it right. Franklin Douglas sells dime bags over on MLK, you no History Channel having bitch."

"Whatevs. Ain't nobody got time for that; I ain't gonna be on no game show. I got all the learning I need to get this job done, so shut that shit up. We 'bout to get paid, so keep your shirt on."

"My shirt is on. Pants on, too. You got my ass up and out the crib bright and early this morning, dog, dragging me down here in your raggedy ass Corolla. And this is what we come for? To watch these illegals do some work?"

"Yo, Haze, just keep it up and you ain't getting shit. Now just hold up one sec and keep an eye out for a plain white van - no windows. That's what we looking for. They come early to keep it on the down low."

Damien pushed Haze back against the white trailer and crouched at the corner, his eyes aimed at the construction scene at Harbor Point. He glanced at his watch, a scuffed Casio that was always five minutes fast, and then turned to his cell and poked in a text. "Keep a lookout. I gotta check in with the pussy; make sure we got a place to crash after this hit."

Alex "Haze" Haywood frowned over Damien's shoulder and stared through the fog at the motley worksite. The morning was dark enough without the fog, and with clouds dominating the sky, there was no sun in the forecast. Haze yawned as the already bustling 27-acre site began revving up for the day. From his vantage point at the south end of the ocean of asphalt, he counted a few dozen workers in pale blue coveralls just like the ones he and Damien were wearing - same orange hard hats, too. They moved like ants between the trailers and the massive cranes and other machines with a lack of intensity, an attitude he recognized in himself now. It had been a hard night. He and one of the waiters had been stuck after hours with a grease spill in the kitchen, pulling double duty when the kitchen staff came up short-handed. But they'd righted the ship with a sort of focused ballet of buckets and mops. Here was that same sort of choreography, only in slow motion - the caffeine hadn't kicked in yet.

It reminded him of the football field at Baltimore City College, where he earned the nickname "Hazard". Those early morning practices had been painful, but he'd racked up a state record in rushing yards for a quarterback, and that had been worth it. That was, of course, a long time ago, before blowing out his knee, the gangbanging and the two years in the city detention center. He'd lucked out and got the job at The Artisanal, where he'd been for over a year, but now here he was with Damien again on "a job".

Haze closed his eyes and threw up a silent prayer - this was the last time, he promised. The last time.

Boom!

The very air vibrated around them, shocking Haze out of his reverie, sending him crashing back against the wall of the trailer. The ground was still shaking from the tremor, and for a moment Haze remembered the earthquake that had jolted the Charm City just a few years prior. He gazed out across the empty lot for an escape route, wondering where the best place to be was in case the disaster ratcheted up, but Damien's quiet laughing pulled him around, anger clouding his face.

"The fuck, D?"

"Pile drivers. They building shit. They driving them big ass metal poles in the ground."

"You weren't gonna tell me? Scared the shit out of me." Haze kicked at Damien, caught him in the shin, but Damien kept laughing and stood up, slipping his cell into his back pocket.

Boom boom! A second pile driver went to work and the air was filled with twice the thunder, a storm that seemed to grow as each new piece of machinery began to move.

"Nah, I was holding out on you. Wanted to see you jump. You always so fucking cool and shit." He winked and peeked around the corner. "So, anyway, yeah. They started this job three weeks ago. Putting the foundation down now, but they can't dig 'cause of the toxic waste down there. You know, that old plant and all that was here long time ago. Shit'll kill a nigga, I guess. So, they all putting in these metal poles to keep shit stable - whatever, some construction shit. Like a earthquake all day here."

"So, what does this have to do with us? I told you already; I got a job. And it don't require me to wear no hard hat and coveralls."

"Yeah, but ain't no paper in cheese and wine, and muthafuckas here get paid. In cash." He turned back, grinning, his one gold incisor gleaming. "Cash, motherfucka. All those muthafuckas out there is illegals - cheap workers, got no checking account, not on the books. They get paid in cash on Friday, and it's muthafuckin Friday right now." He grinned again, his big mouth stretched like a Cheshire Cat, his dark skin like a shadow against the backdrop of the white metal trailer. "Know what that means? Pay day."

Haze shrugged. Shit happens - he'd told himself that a million times, and this was another of those times. Things were going well, and D was always trouble, but maybe they would make out this one time - a little seed money for that cooking school, which was a few thousand even with financial aid. Just one more time with Damien, and then he was the fuck outta there, Charm City or not, it'd begun to lose its luster, it's charm. Muthafuckas never left the ghetto in Baltimore - born in the hood, die in the hood - but Haze was having none of that. He just needed a little something to get him over the hump, and then he was on his way to being a chef.

"Pay day." Haze looked back around the corner of the trailer, took it all in, felt the ground moving beneath his feet. "Bet," he said. "What's the plan?"

"A'ight. Here we go. White van - payroll. Comes in between six and six thirty every Friday morning."

"How you know that?"

"You don't wanna know. Don't ask questions unless it's 'What do you want me to do, D?', a'ight? Too many questions get a nigga killed. You know the rules. So just roll with it. We don't wanna damage that pretty butterscotch skin of yours that all the white girls in Canton want." Damien rolled his eyes, then peeked around the corner of the trailer again before Haze could respond.

Haze's eyes followed. No van yet. Workers worked; pile drivers piled. The eastern sky was edging towards a lighter shade of gray now, and the air was filled with a mist that blanketed the whole worksite and gave it a ghostly aspect - perfect cover for a snatch-and-run. And they had their disguises on, and the car was close-by. Haze took a deep breath.

"It's gonna storm soon."

"We'll be outta here by then," said Damien, pulling out two pistols from the pockets of his coveralls. "We each have a gun and a mask."

He handed one of the black 9mms across to Haze and produced a pair of surgical white masks from another pocket.

"We don't shoot nobody."

"Not unless some muthafucka wants to be a hero. Just point it at his ass, and he piss himself and give us what we want. Cool?"

Haze looked down at the gun - it felt a little too heavy. But damn, it was seed money. Just a little seed money. And weren't the dudes here paying illegals? Cheap fucks. He'd read the news, heard all about the protests over this site and what could happen if they crack open the cap that sealed off the toxic waste. Haze wasn't the ignorant one in this caper. But maybe he was if he was following Damien into an armed robbery. What was next? He took a deep breath. Seed money - he told himself. Seed money is all a brotha needs sometimes.

"I don't want the gun, D."

"Keep it. Makes ya look fierce. You ain't gotta shoot shit. We just gonna ask nicely for the cash and walk away. And won't nobody know who we are; all these muthafuckas is wearing masks right now 'cause of the dust. We just workers. The van rolls up, and we walk across to the payroll trailer. Smooth, now. No hurry. We just working here. They drop the money in the safe and exit; we roll in and take it. One dude in there. We take the money and come right back here. Nobody knows shit. Nobody sees shit. Nobody hears shit. And we out. They gonna think it was some Mexican took their shit."

"What's the take?" Haze licked his lips.

"Ah yeah, boy," said Damien smiling again, nodding his head. "He's in. A'ight, Haze. I knew you was the right nigga for the job. It's fifty k, I hear. Five-Oh big ones. Ten for you; ten for me; thirty for the muthafucka that put me on this and got me the costumes and guns."

"Inside job."

"Damn straight. Only way to go." Damien laughed again, then turned and peeked around the corner just as a white van pulled up to the trailer they'd been watching. He pocketed the pistol and slipped the mask on until the only thing showing was his eyes. "Let's go, Haze. Gear up. It's get paid time. We about to get paid. Then we's getting laid."

Haze swallowed, followed suit, and a moment later they were rounding the corner of the trailer, headed for a payday. It looked to be about fifty yards of asphalt between them and the money, and he couldn't help but see the field in front of him and assess the defense. It was in his blood, and it had been a long time since he'd run all out. What would be his forty-yard clock now? His hundred? Could he even move like he had, take a hit, or was he soft now? It'd only been four years, and he was still in the prime of his life, just going nowhere, looking at a life of food service or some other shitty career if that was the right word for it.

The college recruiters had stopped calling after that night in Montebello Park, where Jimmy Jr and Mikey got popped, and Haze had been able to outrun everyone except the BPD. And that was the end of his football career, the end of the dream, and the beginning of a new life minus the college offers, the Heisman, and the Rookie of the Year award in the NFL. It all ended in a flash, a gun he never had, trouble that he didn't ask for, and a brother that he couldn't protect. Just like that - gone.

Now he was here, and the van was pulling away. It was time for another new chapter, and what it held he couldn't say. He looked up at the gray clouds and shrugged. Game time.

Damien bounded up the steps and caught the edge of the door before it closed, his hand in his pocket with the pistol. Haze was right behind him, pocket still heavy. Plain gray filing cabinets rattled just inside the door of the on-sight office, and an oscillating fan hit them square in the face with cool air just as a wide body stepped into their path. A big fucker, rolls of fat maxing out his dirty shirt and bulging at his neck, stepped forward, making the floor tremble, hand out and pushing into Damien's chest before he'd taken two steps.

"Hold on, amigo!" he bellowed. "Where the hell do you two think you're going? The 'breako trailero' is next door, and it's not break time. Comprendo?"

Damien wasn't fazed for a moment. He swatted the fat paw away, his right hand coming up behind it like a boxer, only in the place of a heavy bag glove there was a matte black Glock 9mm, its squarish muzzle pressing into the fleshy cheeks of the fat man. "Comprendo, puta. You?" It was about as much Spanish as he knew, but it was effective enough as "Lamar", according to the name stitched into his blue short-sleeved shirt, backed up, his hands shaking as they simulated the universal signal for a touchdown, revealing stained pits and a stink that should have been reserved for the end of the day, not the beginning. "Back up, muthafucka, and get over to that safe. It's payday, and we need an advance." Lamar nodded and did as he was told, his eyes wide now, bottom lip quivering.

Haze hung back, watching the door, pulling it tight and locking it. Now was not the time to encounter another legit member of the work crew. His gun was solidly in his pocket, and that's where it would stay if he could help it. The only threats he ever wanted to issue were the kind that came with his Nikes firmly on green artificial turf. The rest he would leave to D, who seemed to be doing fine without help.

The fat man was on his knees now, bent over the floor safe, the crack of his ass mirroring the new day that was slowly creeping up on them outside. He fingered the electronic lock, and with a bit of a relieved flourish, he twisted the simple black handle and pulled the door open. Damien shoved him out of the way the moment he saw the two black bags. He yanked them up and dropped them on the floor. Before they'd even settled, he had a zipper in hand and then a handful of greenbacks that reflected the smile on his face. "Jackpot, baby!"

Haze turned, his eyes lingering for a moment on the money, the future, the chance he needed now more than ever, then he froze as the fat man behind Damien clawed his way to his feet and lurched over the desk, his fat ham hand reaching for something. "Damien!"

But it was too late. "Comprendo this, hombre," the guy growled, and slammed his paw down on the big red button set into the wall next to the lamp, setting off an ear-splitting claxon inside the flimsy aluminum trailer.

Then his face exploded in a shower of blood, and he slumped to the ground.

Haze felt more than heard the shot, watched Damien turn, the barrel of the Glock smoking, his face masked in fury, fifty-dollar bills fluttering to the floor next to what had been Lamar.

"Fuck, D!" The words were just out of Haze's mouth when the whole trailer seemed to come off the ground for a moment and then crash down again, sending him sprawling, scrambling out of the way of a falling cabinet, wondering for a second if someone had come bursting through the door and bowled him over. But when he looked up, there was nothing but the blaring alarm, the red light over the door whirling, and all three of them on the ground. Damien was looking his way, this time with less of a sure fire in his eyes, his pistol aimed now at the door.

"What the fuck was that?"

"Dunno," said Haze, glancing up at the door then back at his friend. "You tell me. You said no muthafuckas was getting shot, D. What the fuck was that?"

"Shit happens," said Damien, snarling as he looked around for more threats. "Now we gots to go. I didn't know there was gonna be no alarm." He scrambled around, gathering up loose fifties.

"That was some vital shit to know or not know," said Haze as he dropped to his knees to help. "Anything else we oughta know?"

Damien pretended not to hear or was just ignoring his friend, eyes on the money, zipping up the bag. "We cool when we walk out, hear? Frosty." He stood and tucked the gun away in a pocket.

"Like you was so frosty." Haze was up now, too, checking the gun in his pocket, watching the door. Was Five-Oh already out there? Were they forming up just waiting for the two fools who robbed the payday to come out? Would he get a lighter sentence since he hadn't pulled his pistol at all? Was he about to test his forty again, that knee? And could he outrun a bullet? There was nothing to do for it now. It was done, and he'd been the dumbass to go along. Just a little seed money. Damn. This was real jail time - armed robbery, and that was that.

Hand on the doorknob, Haze felt Damien fall in behind him. He grabbed his share of the load and slung the strap over his shoulder, then yanked the door open and prepared to face the music, hands ready to go sky high, no gun bullshit. Only there was nothing waiting, no small army of Baltimore bluecoats hunkered down behind black and whites, no hovering ghetto birds, no barking from a bullhorn. There was only a hazy sunrise looming over the high rises that dotted Harbor East - that and a silence that was as eerie as it was unexpected.

The low, thudding roar of the piledrivers was gone, and the entire worksite seemed to be waiting for something like a graveyard expecting a funeral procession. Haze looked left and right, his eyes finding a few workers standing around as if suddenly unsure of what they'd been tasked to do, as if they instinctively knew that no payday was coming, and so there'd be no work coming for the day in return. But there was something else, something he could feel, something that kept him from following Damien right away and left him standing next to the scene of the crime.

It started as a low rumble, as if the city was coming back to life and had begun to breathe again, and then he felt it in his Nikes, heard it building in the creak of the trailer walls, the yawn from the steel latticework of the looming tower cranes. Haze looked at Damien, who had stopped and was looking back, then he began to run.

Then the ground shifted, sending them both flying.

2

"WHAT WAS THAT?" JESSIE rolled over and peeked past Rick's shoulder to the dark window. "Did the building just move or did you just fart?"

Rick groaned and rolled over onto his stomach, slid his hands up under the pillow and went silent.

Jessie eyeballed him and frowned. It'd been a long night, and he'd taken it on the chin with the whiskey shots just before closing. Again. It was a ritual, of sorts, but then they'd let Johnny and Misha and Roxie stay after closing. Again. More shots and more shots, and then the cots in the back for all three of them. Again. Shit was getting old, maybe it was just her. Speaking of which, they'd need to get those three out of that back room and prep before lunch. Romero would be in to get the kitchen going around nine, along with Jose and Chico, and he would be all over them all day if the place wasn't spotless and ready.

Jessie shifted and swung her legs around, sitting up and stretching. Her hips were tight - fucking Rick and his *whiskey dick!* It wasn't stereotypical; it was amazing. It was better than the little blue pill any day, but it made walking difficult the morning after. She turned and let her eyes wander over the sleek, muscular back of her favorite bartender and boyfriend, and imagined him leaning over her, the muscles in his shoulders flexing and the cute way his butt tightened up when he thrusted into her...or Roxie that one time they'd invited her up. His ass looked amazing, but...

She took a deep breath, running her fingers through her dirty blonde rat nest. It was knotty and tangled and she loathed the brushing - why didn't she just get it all cut off and be a pixie like Roxie? Maybe because Rick liked something to pull on. She frowned, images flooding her head. Maybe because he'd liked fucking Roxie a little too much.

"Wake up, dick."

"It's Rick," said a muffled voice from deep inside the pillow.

"Yeah."

"Time is it?"

Jessie glanced at the clock and groaned. "Six."

"Why are you awake?"

"I don't know. I felt something, didn't you? Or maybe I dreamed it. I was having the weirdest dream. We were eating crabs - picking 'em apart, and suddenly they came alive and started chasing and killing everyone. What the fuck is that?"

"Jesus, Jessie." Rick half rolled over and fixed a single open eye on her. "Maybe you need to lay off the Jim Beam."

Jessie looked back and screwed up her face, made a fist and pretended to punch him. "Pow."

"But damn you look hot in the morning, baby. Come put that hot little body on me." He twisted the rest of his body around and pulled down the sheets, revealing a full-sized anaconda and a sly smirk. "Morning wood is the best."

Jessie giggled and turned, climbing onto all fours. "I'm not sure if I can take another dose of that cobra venom so soon, but I think I have a remedy for what ails you."

"Ricky!" The voice came from the front room, and before Jessie could even turn around, a familiar face peeked around the bedroom door. "You're up!" Roxie pushed through the door in her panties and tank. "Bathroom's free."

Fuck! Jessie spun, a scowl dropping across her face like the final curtain, and covered up. Fuck, she thought, fuck. How much Beam did we have? She scrambled off the bed and reached for Rick's gray hoodie that was on the floor. It was her go-to.

"But didn't you feel the quake?" she said and jumped into the spot vacated by Jessie, looking from one to the other.

Rick just laughed. "Both of you need to lay off the booze. Another round and you'll be seeing fire rain down from the heavens or the seas boiling over."

Jessie watched helplessly as her hand came up, middle finger extended.

Rick laughed again and propped his head up with a hand, his eyes having lost sight of his girlfriend, fixated on the way Roxie's shirt bulged in front. A quick glance back at him, his dick still erect and visible, told Jessie exactly what she needed to know, and she slipped the hoodie on, pulling it down over her waist and those bits that had been intended for Rick. "I'm getting coffee," she grumbled and pushed past Roxie without a second look.

It was her own fault, she told herself. She'd let it happen, but what a fake bitch! It was obvious why she tried to stay late every weekend now. Ever since that one night when they'd played Truth or Dare Shots after Johnny had passed out in the back and Misha had gone home, she's been gunning for his wang. And fuck, again? And again and again. It was supposed to be a one-time thing.

Glaring at the world and trying to ignore the giggles that came from the bedroom, Jessie stomped across the carpeted floor in her bare feet and tapped the power button on the coffee maker. She eyed it when it guffed with a sudden cloud of steam, wondering if she should just rip it out of the wall and throw the old clunker away - poor Mr. Coffee was on his last legs - or if she should wait until the coffee was made and then take it back into the bedroom and dump the whole thing on that bitch and the guy she'd wondered more and more lately how to keep interested. How could she compete with Miss Double-E's porn star? No doubt, she was topless and giving him a show, probably even stroking that fat snake.

Is that how shit was gonna be? Had she done that by just opening the door once?

"Fuck you both," she grumbled.

"What?"

Jessie turned and sighed - another uninvited guest. It was high time they stop letting these fuckers stay the night - all of them. "Nothing." Or at least they should lock the doors to the upstairs.

It was Johnny, and he looked like runny eggs. He smelled like them, too. Scraggly beard and dark hair down to his collar, matted on the side of his face with a cowlick like a chicken wing sticking out in one direction - that's what seemed to be tilting him to one side, or maybe it was the whiskey. He stood there in his gray Thundercats tee and crunchy jeans like some exotic mold growing from the wall. His eyes were riveted on the old industrial-sized Mr. Coffee. He inhaled and offered her as much of a smile as he could muster. "Coffee. My kingdom for a cup."

"Well, I don't know if I can take your entire exterminating business in trade for just one cup of coffee, King Arthur, but that's quite a deal you're offering." She turned her back to him - he was painful to look at, and he was first on the donor list for a new deodorant and zit cream - and reached up into the cabinet over the coffee maker. The over-sized cups clinked together and thudded a little too loudly on the faux granite countertop. Each read "Eat at Bertha's" in a comic sans-like font, and each held an orgasmic amount of coffee, which Jessie began to pour. When she pushed the giant pot back onto the warmer, she looked back at Johnny and nodded, then scooped up her cup and swung around.

"Milk and sugar in the usual places?"

Jessie ignored him; he knew where they were. What she needed to know was where Roxie's mouth was. And yet she knew. It wasn't the first time since they'd invited her up that one night, and now, well, how to say, "No more"? She'd let it happen. She'd said it was okay and went along to make him happy. And now....

Her hand trembled and the coffee sloshed against the sides of the cup. "Shit!" She set the cup down as fast as she could on the counter, the hot liquid splashing over the lip, but it wasn't her hand that was trembling, not anger bubbling over that caused the momentary burn. The whole fucking building seemed to move. Then everything went still. Was she just imagining this?

But Johnny was staring at her, two yellow packets of Sucralax poised between his fingers, eyes wide, his mouth moving for a moment, nothing coming out.

"Um." It was all she could manage.

"I thought it was just me, but... Did you feel it earlier, too, or am I getting the shakes again? I figured it was just me." He stood there, frozen, waiting for a response, some kind of answer to his question or for another tremor, then he blinked, seemingly coming back to reality, and recognizing the sugar packets waiting. "I'm gonna need more coffee than this, or maybe we're going to have to open another bottle of whiskey."

"Or both."

"Or maybe we skip the coffee."

Jessie nodded, wiping her hand on the hoodie. It wasn't hers anyway, so fuck it. "We had that quake like a few years ago, remember? 'Never forget?' That was so funny, except it wasn't funny at the time. But what about now? That was a tremor, right? Right?"

She glanced down at the coffee again, hesitant to pick it up, but needing its dark roast goodness more and more with each passing moment. Then suddenly, it came back, the floor shuddering, the cup rattling against the hard faux oak of the table. Then silence and stillness. Then before she could even blink, it came back again, a lurch that launched her coffee cup onto the floor with a dark brown splash and a dead thud. Jessie squealed and leaped out of the way to save her toes.

"Earthquake!"

Jessie spun back to the scream and watched Johnny toss his cup into the sink, where it shattered. Then, he turned, shirt stained brown down the front now, and ran for the door, Jessie right behind him. But she stopped just as quickly as the ground steadied underfoot, listening to Johnny's thudding footsteps on the stairs. She looked down at herself and frowned. No pants, no shoes, no nothing. Earthquake or not, Fells Point or not, she wasn't running out of the damned door onto Bond Street with nothing but a hoodie on. Swallowing against the urge to just run, she turned back to the bedroom at a fast walk, the closed door and what was behind it no longer a concern. They had to get out before...the floor shuddered again, then groaned, then seemed to jump in the air, sending the long-legged blonde catapulting in through the bedroom door. She came down on all fours, ending the morning like she started it. She crawled forward, her breaths coming in shallow and rapid, and pulled herself to her feet at the foot of the bed, where she found the rest of her world undone, Roxie naked and Rick on top of her, hitting it like a champ, both completely oblivious to what was going on around them. She stared, fixated by the way his ass tightened with each thrust, her stomach twisting into a knot as he grunted like a pig and the bitch thrashed with each stroke.

Then Jessie snapped back to reality and slammed the bed with her fist.

"Earthquake, you assholes!" she said, her voice booming across the small room, drowning out the building's own groan, and then she was down again as the ground skipped and bounced her to her knees right next to yesterday's heap of clothes. Rick bounced up and off the near side of the bed; then Roxie hit the floor next to him, her eyes suddenly alert and aware, terror gripping her and drawing her mouth open for a scream, but Jessie stopped her in her tracks with a hard slap, whipping the brunette's head around. "That's for fucking my boyfriend, you bitch. Now get your clothes on and get the fuck out of here before this fucking place crashes to the ground."

Whatever the "Earthquake of 2012" had been, it had been nothing like what was happening now. Wave after wave of shocks ripped through the building, bouncing the three in the bedroom off the floor, then sending them sprawling and scrambling for anything and everything. Roxie's shrill screech drowned out the death throes of their little abode, adding to the chaos and Jessie's pounding head. She snagged her jeans and socks between aftershocks, desperate to be out of the building and away from the screaming, pulled on her boots, then skittered across the floor like a spider and snagged her t-shirt off the doorknob, where it still miraculously clung. Her phone bumped around on the floor like a child's toy next to the dresser, but with a little effort she managed to scoop it up and get out into the living room.

"Wait for us!"

Jessie ignored the plea, unsure whose voice was behind her as the house twisted, and the bedroom door slammed shut. Then the world went still.

"What the...?"

She looked back from her knees, but no one was there. Somewhere behind the door she could hear screaming Roxie and Rick's voice saying something. No doubt he was wiping her tears away while probably trying to hold both her tits in his hands. It was a picture that came through loud and clear, one that gripped Jessie's stomach and squeezed it again, wringing it out like a wet dish rag. Hadn't she always tried to make him happy? And now he was in there banging that bitch out while she made the coffee and tried to warn them about an earthquake? Or was she blowing this all out of proportion? After all, it had been her idea to let Roxie come upstairs with them that one time; she'd been hinting at Jessie that whole night anyway, and Jessie hadn't been left out at all. Still, she felt sick, and now. Now what?

"When a threesome doesn't involve one of the three, it's not a threesome anymore." Her sister had told her that when they'd talked on the phone. "Be careful," she'd said. "Love ya," and then she'd hung up.

Jessie stared at the phone now, the world suddenly quiet and peaceful again. She tapped the screen and saw the pic of Rick and her wrapped up in each other's arms, throwing some bullshit gang signs - no doubt drunk. The picture was her profile picture now - social media love. Her whole life was wrapped up in this little apartment. The bar was downstairs - shortest job commute time in Maryland. They were a dynamite bartending tandem; the three awards no longer hanging from the walls attested to that. But maybe that was a sign. She looked over at the three simple plastic frames that held their certificates from the last three years: Best Bartending Tandem - City Paper. And who could beat a team that lived and worked together and had some kind of extra-spacial perception - *ESP,* she called it - always moving effortlessly and fluidly behind the bar at One-Eyed Mikes? They'd been unstoppable...until now.

When the door swung open, Roxie came crawling out, her cutoffs in one hand and her top in the other. There were tears gleaming in her eyes. "We're going to die. We're going to die," she said between long, wracking sobs. "We're going to die!"

She moved slower than most cows, Jessie thought. They'd have to put her out to pasture sometime and see. Bitch.

Rick was right behind her, ballcap and jeans and boots already on, t-shirt hanging from one hand. For a moment, Jessie couldn't help but see what she'd been gushing after for a little over a year now. He looked downright heroic standing there. Rugged. His chiseled chin was destined for a magazine cover or at least a RoFo ad, and his abs, while not as etched as they once were, still could catch a girl's eye faster than a great pair of shoes.

"Let's go. We've got to get out of here before another aftershock comes through. These old ass buildings can't take it." It was in these moments, when he was being forceful and take-charge, that his Texas drawl came through. Or when he was really drunk and whispering sweet nothings in Jessie's ear. Or Roxie's. Now, that twang pulled Jessie's eyes up from his abs and had her focusing and listening and scrambling to her feet.

She threw on her clothes like a pro, pulling the hoodie back on over top of everything. She whipped the hair tie off her wrist and pulled her rat's nest back into a manageable ponytail, then looked down at the blubbering cow on the floor, then back up at Rick. "I'd say that one's all yours, Cowboy. I'll be downstairs." She flipped him the peace sign coupled with a flash of icy death in her eyes, and turned to go, ignoring Rick's voice at her back, her name on his lips. He had some 'splainin' to do, some serious ass-kissing, a host of "I'm sorry" cards and flowers to send before she was hearing another word. And that bitch had to go. Today was the end.

Jessie's daypack was by the door, so she was set. She unzipped it and double-checked the contents. Wallet, chapstick, tampons, flip flops, O's cap, Sig Sauer P229 - everything a girl needs to be ready for a night out or a natural disaster - sometimes they were the same thing. She pulled the fridge open and snagged two bottles of water and tossed them into the pack for good measure, then zipped it back up and slung it over her shoulder. She was ready for any nightmare.

She turned back once more to watch Rick bent over trying to console his new personal fuck toy, get her dressed and moving, then she spun back to the door and reached for the knob just as the room tilted, and her whole world turned upside down.

3

"UP, HAZE, UP!"

The voice was far away, but no less filled with urgency. A dream that screamed for him to wake up, an alarm that drew Haze out of a dream and into a nightmare. He blinked, took a breath and coughed.

"Up! Let's go, Haze. We gots to go!"

"What?" It was the only word he could manage through the chest-heaving hacking as he climbed to his hands and knees, pushing up from the asphalt into a cloud of dust. The left side of his face throbbed; his shoulder on that side tweaked, too. "What happened?"

"Who cares! Let's go." Shoes suddenly appeared in front of Haze, and he looked up at his friend, saw the blood on his face. Damien leaned on his knees and coughed, then groaned and tapped the bridge of his nose tenderly. "Fuck," he said through gritted teeth. "Gotta go. Gotta go. Five-oh gonna be coming soon, Haze. Just get up."

Haze blinked again, trying to clear his head, reached for his face, felt the welt there on his cheek, the burning skin, but his hand came away clean - no blood. The shoulder ache felt familiar - just like the few too many hits he'd taken on his non-throwing arm, blind-side blitzes that had dislocated it twice. But it wasn't dislocated now; just aching and in need of some ice. That much he knew. What had happened? Well, that was a different story.

He climbed to his feet, head down, wobbly at first, following Damien, who seemed unwilling to wait a second longer. They needed to get as far away from the trailer as possible. They had the money, and there was a dead body back there. That was armed robbery, and they were fucked if they didn't get gone quick. "Don't do it; that's five to

20

ten, nigga" he mumbled, remembering something Dave Chappelle had said once. Damien ignored him, kept walking, the black bag slung over his shoulder. They crossed the foggy expanse of blacktop at a steady but deliberate pace, cool as shit - just a couple of workers heading to another trailer, then they rounded the corner of the trailer and paused, Haze sidling up next to Damien, who was bent over again coughing and dabbing at his nose with his sleeve.

"Fucking broke my nose. Shit hurt."

"Check your vag at the door, D. Ain't nobody got time for that. You said we gotta go; let's go."

"A second, yo." Damien shook his head. "Seeing stars. Need a sec, yo. Hold ya nuts."

"This shit's all wrong, D. What the fuck happened?"

One moment they were hearing that alarm screaming out their guilt, the next moment the door was open, and they were walking to freedom. Then, out of nowhere the world seemed to cough, and he'd opened his eyes face down on the asphalt. It was like a trap set to go off if the money was taken, but he still had both his legs and the bag full of cash, and not a single person had come after them. No, it was some other shit. Some kind of problem at the work site. Had one of the cranes fallen over, or were the piledrivers all going hard at it, making the world bounce?

Haze drew in a breath and listened. Too quiet now, except for the blustering at his elbow.

"Fuck if I know, Haze." Damien whimpered and leaned up against the flimsy metal of the trailer, tears streaming down his cheeks. He wiped his eyes, sniffled, trying to snort up the blood that Haze knew was there - he'd had enough broken noses over the years, knew how much it hurt.

"Stop touching your fucking nose, D. Shit's broke. Can't do shit with it now. This ain't no fucking movie."

"Yeah, yeah, yeah," said Damien, waving him off. "I know. I know. Just hurts."

"Now maybe muthafuckas in the hood will take you serious since you ain't gonna be so pretty no more," said Haze, cracking a smile.

"Fuck you. Ain't that kinda pretty, but good enough for bitches to grind up on my shit."

"You must not let them see your tore-up ride, and won't nobody be grinding shit if we don't get the fuck outta here." Haze stared at his partner, the smile fading as he looked past him, then around to the expanse of asphalt leading south towards the water and freedom. The fog was still creeping in, swallowing the harbor that was only a couple hundred yards away - already he could barely make out the Frederick Douglas building. The clouds overhead had completely blacked out whatever dawn had threatened, leaving the streetlights' eerie glow the only light. But maybe that was a good thing. No one would find them in this soup.

"Whatcha got?"

"Nothing back there, dog. No one coming after us."

"Nothing? They just back there working?" Damien sniffed again, then he spit out a gob of reddish snot. "Then we gots to go. Muthafuckas is gonna find that fat fuck I wasted sooner or later. Best we be out this bitch before that happens."

"Yeah, nobody coming this way. But," and he paused, that something that was bothering him like an itch he couldn't scratch.

"But nothing, yo. We can get the fuck outta here clean like I said."

"Well, would have been better if you hadn't parked that bullshit getaway hoopty of yours two blocks away." Haze glanced back around the corner of the trailer, suddenly worried again about pursuit. Something was nagging at him, but he couldn't place it. Surely someone had heard the alarm, no?

"That's the plan, yo. I gots a plan. We walk down to the Frederick Douglas place right down there, dump the coveralls and masks in the harbor, just like how we creeped up this muthafucka. Then we walk along the water back to the car. Bam. Shit's fucking foolproof. Even a fool like you can't fuck it up, Haze. Nobody gonna see us down there on the walkway - just runners down there, and them muthafuckers just jamming to they iTunes and on them runner highs and shit. Nobody gonna notice two niggas walking by. Shit. They gonna avoid us, thinking we out to rob a muthafucka anyway. Ain't nobody gonna see shit. So, let's go."

"A'ight," said Haze. He had to admit it was a good plan. The fog made it perfect, and it was definitely gonna rain in a few, washing away any evidence of their escape. As far as they could tell, not one person back at the site had even noticed them going in or coming out. He took one more quick look around the corner, saw nothing, and stopped. That was it - nothing. Nothing was moving. Nothing at all. He froze, then turned back to the site and stared.

"What the fuck, yo? We out this muthafucka. Come on," he said and pulled his mask over his bloody nose.

"Wait, D. Wait. Some shit is going down. See that?" Haze pointed, his finger aiming at the pile drivers he could see through the fog. "Shit ain't moving. Nothing's moving. I don't even hear the alarm now. When did it cut off?"

"So the fuck what, yo? They busted some shit, something broke, made the whole fucking world shake and knocked us on our asses. Works for me. Maybe one of them fucking cranes fell over or some shit like that."

"I dunno, dog. I dunno." Haze stared, waiting, wondering, anticipating something, but it didn't come.

"Ain't shit, yo. Let's go. Gotta go hard. Big dog. Big nuts."

Haze shrugged. Maybe Damien was right, but he couldn't help but feel it, that sensation he had when the blind side backer was coming on a blitz, that something like Spidey Sense that told him to duck, to cover up, to avoid the big hit. Call it what you like, it worked almost every time. Here it was again, that something nagging, tickling his brain - or was that just the fall? Maybe it was nothing at all. Maybe.

At that very moment, he heard the sirens.

"Five-oh!"

They seemed to come out of the mist from every direction - didn't they always? Then suddenly the two friends whirled on the sound as a pair of black and whites appeared out of nowhere behind them on Thames Street and sped around the bend in the road in front of the Frederick Douglas Plaza to the lot entrance, swirling red and blue lights glowing in the fog like purple haze cutting off their escape route. The cars paused at the little entrance shack for the operator to raise the long, metal arm that blocked their way, but Damien wasn't hesitating for a second. He grabbed Haze's shirt and pulled him back the way they'd come.

"Fuck, Haze, change of plans. Let's go." He swept around the corner of the trailer, his broken nose seemingly forgotten.

Haze didn't need any coaxing, but before he could take ten steps, he froze in his tracks as the very ground beneath his feet shifted. Then suddenly the sirens themselves were drowned out as the lot let out its own angry groan, shifting again, trembling, then quivering and quaking. The asphalt rolled under his feet, a liquid wave of black tar, and he reached out for something to grab as the whole world seemed to skip, throwing him to the ground again. He caught Damien's fall out of the corner of his eye, heard his wail, then rolled over onto his hands and knees to try and steady himself, his eyes fixed on the nearby trailer as it shifted and swayed, the sheet metal walls shrieking under the assault like a woman screaming. Just beyond it, the two cop cars had stopped and the officers were falling out of their vehicles, floundering in a sort of comic dance, trying desperately to stay upright as the ground beneath their feet bounced and buckled.

"Fuck, Haze! It's a fucking earthquake!" Damien screamed again, and his body careened against Haze's, bowling him over onto his back.

"Up, dog, up. Run! We gotta to get outta here."

"You get up, yo."

"I can't. Fuck. Fuck!"

Haze threw his arms out, trying to steady himself again, trying to ignore the shit that was coming outta Damien's mouth, even though he agreed. But run to where when he couldn't even get the fuck up?

Then just as quickly as it started, the world went silent and still, leaving the two flat out on the blacktop, Haze dragging in deep breaths, Damien wheezing through his ruined nose. They lay there for a few seconds, each looking at the other, then Damien grunted and pushed himself up on all fours. Haze followed suit, his eyes scanning the fog, then turning back towards where he'd last seen the cops. They were still there, all four of them, laid out on the asphalt, too, like they'd been spat out of the cars. They were moving now, trying to get up, and that was all the motivation Haze needed to climb to his feet and snatch the black bag up and pull it over his shoulders.

"Get moving, dog," he said, his voice low as if the fog would carry the sound across the suddenly quiet lot.

"No way. We stick with the plan. We got guns, bitch."

"Fuck no, you ignorant mothafucka," growled Haze, grabbing Damien and spinning him around. We walk out. You ain't shooting shit. I ain't going out like that."

Damien stared, his eyes as hard as Haze's eyes, but he blinked first and nodded. "A'ight."

"Through the construction site, D. Straight through north to Lancaster. Just look like you s'posed to be here. Then we headed for the car the roundabout way. Got it?"

"Bet."

Haze nodded and followed Damien back towards the trailer they'd just left, back towards the scene of the crime, which was now looking much worse for the wear, one end of the trailer sagging on its supports, and even worse, the door of the trailer hanging open at an odd angle.

He tried not to look, tried to pretend it was nothing, tried to pretend that his heart wasn't racing. Maybe no one would be able to see in there and see the dead body from the doorway; he couldn't look. As they passed it, he kept his eyes on the ground in front of him, lest he somehow give it away. Within a few seconds, they were past it and among a group of potential co-workers, a nervous buzz of Spanish, and an even thicker mix of fog and dust, tinged with fear.

"Just keep moving," he mumbled to himself, knowing the cops were behind them somewhere. He was just waiting for the alarm to sound again, for voices to bark out that classic "Freeze, nigga!" that he'd heard that one time before. Would they shoot? Would he shoot back? Or just run? Or was there really any way to get away with a gym bag full of money and a head that still felt a little like he had a concussion? He had the stamina, but did he have the balls? Those weren't linebackers in pursuit. And could Damien keep up?

Questions swirled around Haze's head like the palatable fog. It was only a matter of time before they were answered, and he could feel the sudden, familiar burst of energy expanding from his chest and tingling in his fingertips, that feeling he'd get before each game, each half, each snap. It was time to ball, and Damien or not, he was going for the end zone. No jail for this baller, he thought. Ain't happening. Just the dough, the seed money, what brought him here and what was going to take him away from it all and give him that one new chance he needed.

"Attention all workers. This is the police."

A voice rang out somewhere behind them, a boosted, electric-sounding voice from a megaphone or some kind of PA system. Feedback creaked from the speaker, an ear-splitting shriek that made Haze wince, but he kept moving past a crowd of workers at the base of one of the pile drivers. It sat silent, one of the massive contraptions that had scared him the first time it cranked up and shook the ground with its hammer thuds. The workers buzzed with nervous energy, hushed voices and subtle hand movements. It was all Spanish, which did nothing for Haze, and they never looked his way, so he ignored them and kept going. Just past the pile driver, he scooted right, trying to put it between him and the cops. They'd just crossed into the main construction area, masks on, hard hats and coveralls just like everyone else, but a long way to go still to get through to the other side and then what looked like a football field of asphalt to the fence on the north side.

"This shit ain't gonna work, D."

"Shut it, yo," hissed Damien, and he kept walking.

"Attention all workers. You are ordered to stop all work immediately and gather here at the foreman's trailer. Officers will be conducting a search. A crime has been committed, and anyone attempting to flee will be arrested. I repeat - this is the Baltimore police, and you are all ordered to come forward in an orderly fashion."

Before Haze had even taken two steps, the whole lot erupted in chaos, and he almost laughed when Damien broke out into a run. Illegals - he'd said they were mostly illegals, and it had to be true because just as soon as the cops stopped talking, everyone ran for it, a hundred or so identically dressed minions in hats and coveralls, their faces covered by masks, yelling in Spanish passing here and there, but mostly the beating of boots on the pavement and the crackling of the PA system.

"Come back here! Everyone freeze! We're the fucking police! Stop where you are! Come back, goddamnit!"

Haze was right next to Damien, balls out running, and the non-athlete was keeping up pretty good, considering how out of shape he had to be and the fact that his busted nose couldn't be helping. He wheezed and cursed under his breath as they dodged pallets of concrete, scooted between vehicles, and tried to blend into the wave of blue coveralls that washed across the lot. It was going to work. It was going to work, he kept telling himself, and as they passed the last piledriver, he saw the far fence beckoning, the gap in the north end where the little parking lot attendant shack was sitting empty. It was going to work.

Haze smiled, seeing the end zone coming up and nothing but daylight ahead. They'd head up Lancaster, dump the clothes in the cluster of parked cars there, then cruise down Bond to where Damien had parked his Corolla with the spinners on the wheels - ugly piece of shit. But it didn't have to look pretty; it just had to start, which was sometimes an issue. Just this once it had to start, and then they'd be out and counting the money in a parking lot somewhere. And life would be good, and he'd never go back to the hood. From throwing touchdowns to throwing paint on a canvas or a wall - it was a done deal.

Until it was undone with a violent jolt, and the ground beneath them convulsed like a drunk bitch in an alley, throwing them down again onto a blacktop that suddenly opened up in front of their eyes. It groaned and creaked, then cracked like a massive hungry mouth opening and gobbling up a few hapless coverall-clad morsels who'd gotten ahead of Haze and Damien. They screamed as they fell, but the asphalt didn't seem to notice. It groaned again, thunderclap on top of thunderclap, as if a massive storm was ripping through the Charm City. The asphalt peeled back like wrapping paper as the chasm expanded and vomited up a wave of water, a geyser of gray-green gunk, between them and the end zone.

And something else.

"What the fuck?" He could hear Damien screaming as they both tried to scramble away. The ground flipped and twisted, hurling them through the air. Haze came up on all fours, eyes on the prize - the far gate, but it was gone, somewhere beyond the lip of the turned-up asphalt, somewhere past where the others had fallen.

And behind him the air filled with screams and a new sound he couldn't place. He whirled and stared, open-mouthed at what he knew couldn't be real.

4

JESSIE BLINKED AND found herself at the bottom of the stairs, or what was left of them. What they were now was a collection of old wooden planks, splinters threatening to stab her in the eye, and dust clogging her lungs as she struggled to breathe. She coughed through the dust that crowded the narrow landing and pulled sweatshirt up to cover her nose and mouth. Now was no time for decorum; she'd seen enough disaster flicks to know the deal. This wasn't television, like some shitty movie on SyFy.

"I'm okay. I'm okay." she told herself. Nothing really hurt - not a lot anyway, and everything seemed intact and mobile. She'd survived.

And then, "Rick! Rick!" She screamed through the sweatshirt, then pulled it down and screamed the name again. But there was nothing, just the creak of the building, the sounds of movement nearby.

She took a deep breath, inhaling the scent of the man she'd left upstairs, and closed her eyes against any waterworks. He was alive, or he wasn't. That was it, and until she'd made it out of this mess, there was no point in worrying. She swallowed and told herself that it was the only choice she could make for the moment. She'd survived; he would, too. That was that. For now, this was this. She was on the first floor, and there was room to move and air to breathe - at least until there was another tremor or aftershock that brought the whole building down on her and anyone else that might be inside.

Squinting into the swirling darkness, Jessie could just see up what was left of the stairs. About halfway up, the ceiling had completely collapsed, and whatever was beyond that, their little place of residence, was hidden from view - and she thought to herself - maybe not even

29

there anymore. She swallowed and coughed again and pushed that thought away. No way Rick was dead. No fucking way. He was a dick, and his open whore policy had had its day, but he wasn't dead. Maybe just stuck. She needed to find out.

"Rick! Rick! Can you hear me? Are you okay?" She screamed up at the disaster above her, tried to see through the darkness. Nothing came back at her still, just silence and her coughing as she batted at the dust cloud that encased her.

"Rick! Goddamnit, Rick! Are you okay?"

Could he even hear her? She'd screamed as loud as she could; for a moment there she was sure the rest of the ceiling would come down on her in response. Now what? Black visions flooded her head, she swallowed against the panic, suddenly seeing him lying on the floor with some huge piece of debris crushing his body - a beam from the ceiling, a massive chunk of plaster from one of the old walls. He was trapped. He was pinned. He was lying there right now, tears in his eyes, apologizing to her and asking for forgiveness, and she couldn't do anything, even be there to tell him that it was okay, that he was forgiven. It was the oldest lie in the world: everything will be okay. And then the victim dies, and everyone knew it was a lie, but you had to believe it just for the moment, right?

Coughing again, she tried to keep quiet, to listen for a sign, a signal, something that told her he was still alive, but there was nothing, just the building creaking as it settled into its new state and waited for another tremor to send it crashing to the ground. The death blow. She had to get out.

"Help!"

"Rick?" She jumped at the sound and cracked her head on a fallen beam behind her. She winced and doubled over, grabbing at the spot, realizing immediately through the clarity of the pain that it was all wrong. Wrong voice. Wrong direction. Not Rick. He was somewhere else.

"Jess? Jessie, help us! We're back here and we're fucked."

It was Johnny. Someone else had survived.

That was enough to get Jessie moving. She dropped her hand and scrunched down to investigate the semi-blackness in the back of the bar. Somewhere back there, where they usually crashed, Johnny was in trouble. She turned and slid herself along the floor the last few feet, squeezing through a narrow slit between the wall and some debris, until she found herself in the central hallway between the bar and restaurant areas of Mike's. The whole damned thing was choked with blue-gray dust, but at least she could see a little, one of the emergency lights flickering in the corner. She looked front to back, trying to assess the damage, and suddenly everything seemed just a little bleaker. They would not be open for business today or maybe ever. One-Eyed Mikes was marooned, and the crew was in disarray, to say the least.

"Jess? Jess, are you there?"

Johnny's voice, muffled but clear, pierced the quiet again, and Jessie turned, spinning towards the back of the pub to the restaurant section. Somewhere back in the dark was Johnny, and presumably Misha - it was so rare that he left without Johnny.

"Yeah, Johnny? It's me. I'm here. Where are you? I can't see anything back there. Where's Misha?" That was her biggest concern now. Johnny was a young, strong dude, but Misha - he took the term "walking dead" to a new level. Jessie wasn't sure how many times she'd had to put her hand under his nose to see if he was dead or just passed out with his head on the bar again. At his age, it was always in the back of her head. To date, he hadn't died once on his favorite stool, but he'd prayed more than once that he go out that way, making the backwards sign of the Cross every time. But now? There was no telling. He was about as old as dirt, and that didn't bode well.

"He's back here. Keep coming if you can. We're stuck."

His voice warbled as he spoke, not the usual calm, easy-going banter that she was used to with him. She tried to keep her own voice steady - what good would it do to let him know she was just as scared?

"Keep talking." The restaurant portion of the bar was pitch black. The floor dropped about six inches into the dining area, something she was totally ready for because she knew the layout like the back of her hand, but after the quake there was no telling what was in front of her, so Jessie stretched out her hand and shuffled forward like a zombie.

"I'm okay, I think," said Johnny in the distance, but he didn't sound confident. "I think I'm bleeding, or I pissed myself. Whatever it is, it's warm."

Jessie sighed, still holding her sleeve up over her nose and mouth.

"And Misha is down, and I can't tell if he's breathing."

"Okay, I'm coming," said Jessie as she pushed through a mass of chairs and tables that had once looked rustic and charming.

The bathrooms and the kitchen filled the space beyond the tables, but there was a bump-out on the left that served as a service prep area. It was large enough for a few cots. That's where the After-Hours Barstool Gang, as they like to call themselves, usually crashed. It took an excruciating minute or so for Jessie to get there as each table and chair in the place seemed to block her path with splintered wood and jagged stakes only a vampire slayer could appreciate. After a little blind navigation, she felt the floor bump up again to the very back section where the bathrooms and service areas were, and that's where she found Johnny.

He was pinned on the other side of two heavy ceiling beams that gleamed in the only other working emergency light - so much for a real emergency. Beyond them, Johnny's face was like a shadowy mask, his cheeks streaked black. "Careful," he said, his voice wavering. "Every time I try and move, I think everything is going to come down." His eyes indicated the threat, a third beam cracked in half hanging over his head where the ceiling looked primed to collapse.

Jessie swallowed, eyes focused on the danger there, then down at the turn-of-the-century cage Johnny was locked in. How old was the building they were in? Older than her grandfather - that much she knew, but that's as far as her knowledge of the place went beyond how it had been a simple rowhome in a past life. And since the area, Fells Point, had been around since the 1600s, there was really no telling how old those massive beams were or how much more they could take. They made things to last back then...but not to last through an earthquake - they didn't do earthquakes in Baltimore. It wasn't a thing at all.

"And Misha?"

"On the floor here. On my right."

"Is he breathing?"

Johnny just stared, eyes fixed on Jessie's. "I don't think so." It was little more than a whisper. "When it hit, I was trying to rouse him. Drunk old fool. I think the first beam hit him in the head, and it's so dark now. I - I can't see anything."

"But you're okay?" Jessie pointed at the smudges on Johnny's left cheek.

"Yeah, I think so. I don't know if I'm bleeding, but my legs hurt. The floor is covered in something wet; I'm standing in it. I don't know where my flip flops are. I can feel it squishing between my toes. Not cool."

"No," said Jessie, looking down but afraid now to bend down and see what was on the floor. "Can you move?"

"No, I'm stuck, Jessie. You gotta get me outta here. Every time I try to move too much, push one of these beams, it creaks and that scares the shit out of me. I need to get outta here," he said, panic rising in his voice. "Now. Where are the cops? The firefighters? Have you called 911?"

"Shit," said Jessie, fumbling for her phone in her bag. "I didn't even think about it." The light from the phone reflected the tears in her eyes as she dialed, suddenly feeling a little spark of hope, but it faded quickly when the steady beep of the busy signal came back through the earpiece. She ended the call and hit redial only to get the same familiar tone. "Shit, everyone must be calling. This thing must be bigger than I thought."

"That's what she said."

"Ha ha ha - you're so goddamned funny, JohnBoy." There was no mirth in her laughter, but she appreciated how he wasn't panicking.

"Keep calling," was all he said, his voice steady. "Fuck, I'm thirsty. And I think I'm gonna puke."

"It's gonna be okay, Johnny," she said, feeling the lie lingering on her lips. "Just be cool."

The busy tone wouldn't let up, time after time, and finally Jessie gave it up and pushed the phone into her pocket. "It ain't gonna happen, Johnny. Must be cops going everywhere, and firemen, too, trying to dig people out. These old houses; gotta be lots of people trapped." Her eyes roamed back along the darkened path she'd crossed a few minutes earlier. Somewhere back there were the stairs.

"And Ricky and Roxie?"

She shrugged, unwilling to look back at the eyes she knew were staring at her. "They must still be upstairs. I - I don't know."

The room went quiet then, a hush that revealed nothing but slow breaths from the two people waiting and wondering. The emergency lighting in the floors near the bathrooms did little to offer any solutions. It was only powerful enough to reveal the futility of the situation, and no matter how many times Jessie's eyes rolled back to the beams and how they'd fallen perfectly from the ceiling to block in that little nook and trap Johnny, there were no solutions bubbling up in her brain. There was only the nagging feeling that whatever was going on wasn't over yet, the lingering fear of that last beam coming down with the rest of the ceiling, sending them both on to wherever Misha had gotten off to.

"Then, if there's nothing else to do, no one to call, you gotta go get help." Johnny's voice came again, steadier now, pulling Jessie out of her morbid reverie.

"What?"

"You gotta get the hell out of here and get help. Otherwise, I'm just going to be stuck here until the next aftershock and the rest of this wall falls on my head. And yours if you don't get the fuck out of here."

Their eyes locked, and Jessie nodded. There was no arguing about it. Somewhere outside there had to be other people shaken out of their homes, people who could come back and help somehow. That's what people did in community emergencies, right? They got together and helped each other.

"It's the only thing to do. And the sooner, the better, you know?"

Jessie stared at him, through him, to the people she would find out there, people who could not only help pull Johnny out, but people who would help her get to Rick, dick bastard that he was. "Yeah. Yeah, you're right. I'm gonna see if the back door is open, if the kitchen isn't destroyed, and then I'll go out front in the street and see what's what and see if anyone is around, okay? I'll go as fast as I can. I'll be back with help."

"I know. Just go. I'm starting to freak out a little standing here in someone else's blood."

Jessie swallowed as she took one last look at Johnny, then she bowed her head and turned away to the right, towards the kitchen door. It creaked open, and she hesitated, wondering if it would be the straw that broke the proverbial camel's back. Suddenly the whole house sighed, freezing Jessie in place and showering her with dust. She stared at the open door and the darkness beyond, waiting for what would come next, but the house went quiet again, seemingly settled.

"Too late."

Jessie's gaze went back to the hole that was Johnny's current prison, found his eyes riveted on her. The floor was damp, and a pool of reddish liquid was flowing out from underneath the beams.

"Jesus, Johnny!"

"Yeah."

"Were you cut?"

"What? Oh no, I had to piss; I couldn't hold it anymore. Now I'm standing in blood and piss. Can you get a move on and get some help? Um, and another pair of pants for me. I can't run around in a disaster with a crotch stain."

Jessie giggled and offered up a silent prayer. "You are a crotch stain, Johnny. One we can't seem to wash out." Before he could answer, she was through the door, navigating the kitchen, which seemed to be mostly intact. The emergency lighting here was working perfectly. Jessie slipped past the main ovens and the two cooking surfaces she knew intimately thanks to Ricky and some of his after-hours shenanigans. The back door was right where they'd left it, intact and locked. She fumbled with the lock, then the door popped open like it was on a spring, and the morning's light spilled in like a flood of hope. Somewhere out there would be what she was looking for, someone that would be rushing to help when they saw her, and they'd yank Johnny through a wall if they had to, then go looking for Rick and Roxie.

Jessie stepped out into the narrow alley and pushed through the leaning chain link gate to the small parking lot beyond, bounding over the asphalt and inhaling the salt air of the Inner Harbor. It was fishy, but at least it wasn't the stink of dumpster and vomit that was the usual morning calling card. Something to be thankful for, for sure, although there was a definite tang to the air, as if a trawler had come in with a whole catch that'd gone bad already. Plus, there was the whole issue of the fog that blurred everything, and the rain - she blinked against the drizzle when she looked up at the looming clouds, slowing to take it all in, wondering what was coming next, how the streetlights were still on, how the billowing clouds overhead had almost blotted out the glitzy towers of Harbor East only a few blocks away. She could see them moving, like something out of a horror flick, swirling in the air and coming on toward her, hiding some sinister, other-worldly threat. The forecast hadn't said anything about ominous looking death clouds, had it? Her hand tapped the pocket holding her phone, but she let it go. There were other priorities now. The weather would have to wait.

Turning back to the street, Jessie crossed the parking lot quickly, eyes scanning left and right as she came out onto the sidewalk. What she saw there left her gaping.

Bond Street, normally solemn and permeated with the calming aroma of freshly baked bread, bristled with its own agony and anger. Just across from OEM, two of the houses had completely collapsed, flattened as if hit with a wrecking ball. A lone old woman in a bathrobe and slippers was standing in front of one as if she'd just popped out to grab her paper when it fell in behind her. The entire outer wall of The Get Some, a shoddy little bar-slash-club at the corner that portrayed the complete opposite personality of One-Eyed Mike's neighborhood bar personae, had fallen away, its bricks strewn across the ancient cobblestones, the inner workings of the trashy little hotspot exposed to the morning. Down the street towards the water, trees were leaning, centuries old facades had crumbled, and even one Smart Car was overturned like a little mechanical turtle. A small crowd had gathered at the next corner, but none of them were looking up towards the quaint little bar with the city's hottest bartending tandem.

Jessie took it all in with utter disbelief, then turned to find every hope dashed. The second floor of the rowhome, where her little apartment with Ricky was situated, was nothing more than rising dust and fallen roof tiles. Her pack hit the pavement before her butt, and then all she could see were tears.

5

HAZE CHANCED A GLANCE back, saw nothing but the fog billowing, felt the first raindrops across his burning cheeks, and shrugged it off. The sting would wear off; he would live. What he couldn't live with was the vision that now haunted him, that impossible scene only a few blocks away that he was determined to never witness again. What was in front was all that mattered - an expanse of concrete that looked like a trucker's graveyard, and another couple blocks to Damien's car - if it was even still there. The maze of overturned semis and unattached trailers didn't leave him hopeful for an easy getaway, and then he turned the corner on Damien's heels and plowed into his friend, nearly knocking him over.

"What the fuck, D?" he said between breaths. They'd run three blocks, and now they were stopping? "Didn't you see what the fuck is happening back there? We gotta keep moving, dog."

When he turned, glancing over the shoulder of his partner in crime, he saw the flashing lights for the first time and understood. Two black and whites were parked in the middle of Bond Street only a dozen yards away. No officers, but they'd be close by. In fact, just as his eyes left the glare of the lights, an officer came out of a house with an elderly lady waving her phone around. The house next to it was flattened, as were a number across the street.

"Out of the frying pan..."

"...and no chicken box in sight." Damien seemed to snap out of whatever daze he was in, broken nose, earthquake survivor and now staring down the cops with a sack full of stolen paper.

"That's not what I was going for, dog. City's fucking blowing up, and you need some chicken." Haze watched as the cop stopped in the middle of the street with the old woman, then looked up as another policeman emerged from the morning shadows farther down the street. "We gotta go. Five-oh is on the case."

"Oh, no, hell no. Just chill. We regular citizens; just play it cool."

"D, we gotta jet."

"Not yet. I got my eyes on a little something." He looked back and winked, then stepped off.

Just to their left, Haze saw the object of his partner's affection - he'd been too distracted by the flashing lights, but he could see now what distracted Damien: a hot little shorty in a hoodie and jeans, hair up in a ponytail and totally unaware of their presence, or even the presence of the cops, or so it seemed. Her eyes were fixed on the building in front of her, a rowhome converted into a tavern by the looks of it, red and black paint and a sign that looked like a pirate flag and trying to hang on to the building by one piece of chain. The building wasn't totally fallen like the ones across the street, but the top half looked like something really big had sat on it.

"What the fuck," was all that came out of his mouth, and then he was moving forward again, catching up, wondering how Damien's brain worked, or if it worked at all. Pussy and paper; paper and pussy. That's all he saw, even when the whole damned city was quaking and the harbor was flooding into the streets only a few blocks away. And the other. The impossible thing.

"Hey, baby, what's up?" Damien stepped up to the blonde. He should've had his own commercial for those pills that made dicks hard; his always was. Haze shook his head.

When she didn't respond, didn't even look up, he tried again. "You okay, sweet thing? What can Damien do for you today?"

When she looked up, he could see red ringing her eyes. She eyed him up and down, didn't even seem to notice Haze, and then dropped her gaze to her cell phone. "Nothing unless you have tights and cape underneath those overalls."

"Damn, baby, how'd you know? I definitely gots a superpower. You just gotta unlock it."

Haze stopped short, eyes rolling, reminded why he didn't go down on the block much anymore. D was a lost cause, and Haze needed to remember that next time his friend called, but then two words came to mind that shut those thoughts down: seed money. He stared at his friend's back, looked down at the girl there seated on the ground, and shrugged. Five large of those in the bag slung on his back were his, and that was worth a few minutes of Damien's bullshit. Besides, the girl was cute.

And there were four cops in the street behind them now, and one of them was looking their way.

"Yeah, how can we help?" Haze was surprised by his own words, by his own movement as he stepped forward and offered the girl his hand. It went against every instinct - run, hide, get as far away from the cops as possible. But it wasn't going to be that way now. He had to work it and be cool before Damien let too much of his bullshit rap out of the bag and was told to fuck off. Or it'd be ten years for armed robbery and life for murder, even if he didn't pull the trigger. Chappelle had it right.

This chick was a way out.

"My friends are trapped in there." She looked up and gave him a weak smile and her hand.

Haze felt the warmth of her palm and pulled, bringing the ice blue eyes up closer to his own brown orbs. He blinked down at her and swallowed his next words just as Damien stepped in.

"Alright, baby, what you need? Where they at?"

Haze stepped back, let the hand go and turned. He needed a little air. Just help the girl out and go. That's what they needed to do. No need to get caught up in shit. They'd help and go; there was too much at stake to do more. But whoa...she was something alright.

"You sure? My friend, Johnny, is around back. He's stuck and I can't get him out, but maybe you could. I don't know. I -," she hesitated, then started walking around the side, back the way Haze and Damien had come. "Come on. If you're gonna help, let's get to it before the rest of the house falls in and kills him, too."

"Too?" Haze was a step behind Damien, who'd fallen in behind the girl, cutting him off. She led them around the back, leaving the unanswered question hanging in the morning fog. Haze chanced a glimpse toward the cops, and three of them were headed back down Bond Street, the fourth on his radio, watching them.

They tromped around through the parking lot to the kitchen door, where she paused. "Listen, the building fell in when the quake hit, but at least two of us survived - me and Johnny," she said to the door. "Another friend, Misha, was killed by some wooden beams supporting the second floor, the same beams that have Johnny trapped. There's another beam that looks ready to break, and I don't know what to do. It - it's dangerous." With that she turned and looked at them both, her eyes resting on Haze. "I understand if you don't want to risk it. There could be another tremor, and..."

"Shit, girl, maybe you right. We ain't come all this way to end up getting dead like that Misha dude."

Her jaw dropped. Before she could say anything, Haze shoved Damien aside and leaned in. "What's your name?"

"Um, Jessie."

"I'm Haze, and this impolite motherfucker is Damien. We'll help. I just wanted to know your name in case you're the last girl I ever see."

"Yeah, Jessie." She swallowed, still staring at him. "Nice to meet you, and, um, thanks for helping."

"Let's get in there then and see what we can do, if anything, k?"

She nodded and slipped off her backpack, setting it at her feet. "You can leave your bags out here. I'm sure they'll only get in the way."

Haze nodded and dropped his next to hers, but Damien hesitated. "Dude, you sure?" He stared at Haze, then looked at the door long and hard before nodding and then easing his to the ground, too.

"Alright, show us." Haze reached out, laid his hand on Damien's shoulder, and then followed Jessie through the door.

It was dark and dusty inside, a few flickers coming from the emergency lighting. They moved quickly through the kitchen following Jessie's lead and soon found themselves standing in the nook, looking through the dim light into the eyes of the only living soul left in the place. Johnny stared back, silent, waiting.

"It's okay, Johnny. I've brought some friends."

"Friends?" Damien's voice from the rear, causing Haze to roll his eyes again.

"Close enough. Anyone's a friend who'll come into a collapsed building and save a life."

Haze nodded. She had a point. And she'd been totally right about the situation. Johnny was truly fucked.

"You okay?"

"Okay, I guess." Johnny's voice was little more than a whisper. "My legs are numb. I can't feel them. Gotta get me out."

"We're gonna, Johnny. We're gonna."

Then, as if in response to Jessie's challenge, the earth shifted, and the room was filled with shrieking wood and screams. Haze stumbled back, grasping for a handhold on anything, then he crashed to the ground, a soft body falling on top of him, twisting and writhing, and all he could do was hold onto her until the ground stopped moving and things went suddenly quiet.

His heart pounding in his ears, he relaxed his grip on the body draped over him, but she didn't move, her body snug against his, her fingers digging into his skin. He could feel her heartbeat, running like a rabbit against his chest, hear her nasally, ragged breathing between sobs. Trouble - it was the only word he could think of when he opened his eyes and looked down at her. His hand was already stroking her hair, wondering what he could say to get her calm and moving again. Yes, trouble. He'd realized it the moment he'd touched her clammy hand on the street. And now? Well, the first thing they had to do was survive. And then? Well, he didn't need any more trouble.

"What the fuck? Fuck this, dog. I'm outta here."

Haze shook his head, then eased himself up, pushing Jessie up, too. "We're still here. Get up. We're still here," he whispered to her, ignoring his friend who was scrambling around in the darkness nearby. He could see a shadow on the floor, hear Damien grumbling under his breath.

Jessie sat up, trying to wave away the fresh cloud of dust. "Sorry, I..."

"It's cool," said Haze, his fingers brushing hers as he shifted into a sitting position.

"Not cool, dog. Not cool." Damien grunted as he climbed to his feet, followed by the others. "Let's get the fuck outta here, yo. This building coming down on top of us soon. Don't you see?" He gestured at the beam overhead, the clutter of broken furniture and debris. "One more good shake, and we're gonna look like the front of this building, only flatter. I ain't down with that, not after..."

He let the words hang in the air, but Haze knew. He hadn't forgotten what was waiting just outside the door in those bags. First the cops, then the quake, then the pile drivers collapsing around them as the ground at the site split open and the harbor poured in.

"Alright, Let's move it then. We gotta do something fast," said Haze, grabbing the one working emergency light. He swung it on its metal swivel and aimed it at Johnny, stepping up into the nook, but beyond the pale face bathed in sweat, there was nothing but shadows. "I can't see shit. We don't have a -," but his words trailed off when he felt fingers pressing something into his hand. He turned to find Jessie and a yellow Bic lighter.

"I used to smoke. I carry it around now for whatever reason." She shrugged and smiled.

He nodded, his eyes lingering for a moment on her face, then turned and flicked the lighter into action. The flame wavered in the dusty air as Haze pushed his hand forward over the beams and near Johnny's head. It was the only thing he could move, it seemed, and when he did, Haze had his answer. "Damn, that's it."

"What?"

Turning, he grinned and handed the lighter back. "A door. Your boy there is standing in front of a double door."

"Yeah, there's a door," said Jessie, her voice not reflecting the relief in Haze's. "Well, there used to be. It was shut and painted over on this side - you can't really see it, and it was covered over on the outside. I'm sure it hasn't been a door since we've been here, and probably not for a long time. They built the kitchen back there in the Sixties, put the back door in there, so this door probably hasn't been open in... fifty years?"

"Fuck me," came the voice from behind the beams, but Haze wasn't listening. He was already moving, pushing past Jessie and Damien, who were quick on his heels. The kitchen door creaked open again, and the eerie room, littered with the pots and pans and various ruined tools of his dream trade gazed up at him from their scattered places on the floor. At least he could see a bit in here with the outer door open and a little light streaming in. Maybe they could find something.

"What are you doing?" It was Jessie, sliding up next to Haze, closer than he expected when he turned to look at her.

"We need something to get some leverage with, a crowbar, a hammer. I dunno what you got back here. We're not getting him out from this side. We gotta try and go in from the outside."

"I told you those doors haven't been opened in years."

"Wanna get your friend out?" Haze spun on the smaller figure, anger shooting into his voice. Hadn't she gotten them in here? Hadn't she pulled them around to show them this shitshow, and now she was telling him what couldn't be done?

She swallowed and stepped back a bit, eyes on the floor again. "Yeah."

"Then find me something. We'll go outside and pull off that cheap siding or those old bricks and see what we can find. Maybe it's doable. Maybe not. What else we gonna do?"

Jessie didn't offer an answer.

"Then find us something," he said, his eyes drifting up over her head to Damien, who stood behind the girl with that same frown, his hands shoved in his pockets. "I gotta talk to my boy here and get a look at the outside wall. Find something and come out. And hurry."

Jessie nodded as Haze passed her, their eyes meeting again, and then he was gone, pulling Damien after him through the kitchen door into the muted morning light and the eerie quiet of the fog.

"What the fuck, Haze? Let's jet. Fuck these people, yo. We ain't got time for this shit. Look at that there; that's payday," he said, pointing at the black bags at his feet. "And you over here playing savior of the people. Ain't nobody got time for that." Damien was up close, too close, his voice low but his breathing on high, and it was a Cavity Creeps kinda day.

"Check that shit. We stopped when you decided to play Romeo and Juliet, and now you're just sore cause Juliet ain't down. Well, ain't that a bitch, but we do have time for this shit. Because if you remember, there's cops right out there on the street, and they're checking shit out, and don't even think they won't check out two out-a-place niggas in this hood. And what are they gonna find, huh? We got fifty K in paper, and you got a damn piece in your drawers that'll match a dead body less than half a mile from here. Chill, yo, unless you wanna walk out to the street and put on the bracelets now."

Haze stared at his partner, watched the anger seep out of his face, and then all Damien had left were blinking eyes that looked past him to the street. "Yeah, a'ight. Let's get this done, and then we out. Heroes and all; no cops gonna say shit when we walk out with a rescue in hand."

"Bet. Might get a parade and shit later."

Just then Jessie burst through the door, a massive carving knife in hand. "Found something."

"Damn, girl, you packing now? Expecting a heavy crowd for lunch?" Damien backed away from the knife-wielding blonde, a smirk on his face.

"That's all I could find. This isn't Ace fucking Hardware."

"It'll do. Give it over." Haze accepted the knife carefully, gave it a quick inspection, and then turned around to find the spot he was looking for. "D, get in there and talk to our boy for a minute; keep an eye on the place, will ya? Keep him calm, and I'll get to work out here."

There was a grunt of agreement, and Jessie tossed him the lighter. Then Damien was gone, leaving Jessie in tow as they approached the old brick and yellowing siding on the back quarter of the building. He looked left to the door, trying to calculate the distance, and then he stared at the brick in front of him, weighing the glint of the steel against the crusty bricks and mortar. "No way this shit is going to work, you know?" The words came out before he could stop them. His mouth clamped shut too late, and when he looked over at the girl at his shoulder, she nodded.

"I know. I just can't do nothing."

"And to think this is what I've always wanted to have in my hand, only not in these circumstances." He held up what he figured was the number one tool of a chef, a good knife, and when he saw the confusion on Jessie's face, he just shook his head. "Later. Now, I just don't know what to do. I thought; I dunno."

Jessie stood by in silence, her eyes on the solid wall in front of them, and Haze knew what she was seeing: failure. They weren't getting her friend Johnny out, not with a brick wall in the way and nothing but a damned carving knife. The mortar would be solid, and if it wasn't, the wall was gonna come down anyway and maybe end them all. He'd been sure there was something they could do, but...

"Drop the knife. Turn around easy."

The voice came from behind them, and Haze immediately felt the knife slip from his fingers and clatter to the ground. It wouldn't do to turn around with a deadly weapon in hand when Five-Oh was on the scene. Not today; not in this neighborhood; not when you're a black man. This was not part of the plan; he should have stayed in bed.

6

JESSIE TURNED SLOWLY, her hands climbing above her head. "Don't shoot. It's okay. They're with me."

"Chill, fellas. Chill." Haze's voice was lower, not the shrill pleading of the woman next to him.

Suddenly there was a crunch as the kitchen door burst open. Jessie could see the flurry of motion in the corner of her eye as Damien came out, but her eyes were fixed on the two cops and how their guns swiveled with their black clad shoulders to identify the new threat.

"Freeze!"

"Whoa, shit! Cops! Whoa! Whoa! Chill!" Damien's voice was frantic, and his motions exaggerated, hands coming up and waving, palms open to show he was hiding nothing.

"On your knees! All of you. Down. Now."

They moved, eyes glued to the new danger, their mouths frozen open like the end of the gun barrels, but only Damien and Haze dropped to their knees. Jessie ignored them and moved forward, timid steps with her hands still raised. She swallowed hard and finally her voice won through. "It's okay, officers. It's okay. I work here. I live upstairs. Or I did until today."

The lead cop swung around to confront her, his gun still out, but the barrel raised a little skyward now. His green eyes searched her blues, watched her hands. "Hold it, miss. Stay where you are. Tensions are a little high; there's been an earthquake and -."

"No shit, Sherlock." She couldn't help herself, and she bit down the next words that rushed into her mouth before they could find purchase on her tongue. What the hell did they think she was doing here? Looting? This was Baltimore, not New Orleans.

"Hey, we're on the scene to help people and keep order, and you can't exactly say this looks on the up-and-up. You say you work here?" She nodded in response. "Who are these two? Your kitchen staff? Wasn't that guy just holding that rather large knife? A little early morning prep work in the kitchen? You'll pardon me if I think he isn't dressed for the part." The gun was wavering again, this time coming down as Jessie looked on, her arms sliding lower, reflecting the cop's movement, reflecting the aim of the barrel lower and lower until it was pointed at the ground in front of her. A sort of mutual unspoken detente passed between them, but the pistol stayed at the ready.

"I know, officer. These guys were nearby, and they came here to help me. I have a friend trapped right on the other side of this wall, and we were looking for a way to get him out. The other side is blocked, and he's stuck."

"So, you were going to cut him out through a brick wall?" The officer cocked his head; wiped at the pale, wet flesh underneath a shock of black hair. "Is that a Ginsu knife? Light saber?"

Jessie shrugged. "It was all I could find. We don't exactly have the jaws of life in the kitchen. But enough small talk; if you want to help, do you have anything in your car? If we can get through the wall right here, where it used to be the back door, maybe we can get him out." She pleaded, her hands on her hips now - serious business, but the guy on the other end of the gun seemed unconvinced. "Otherwise, go protect and serve those old ladies across the street."

"Dude, come on." Haze had found his voice, but he was still on his knees, hands up. "Let's get to it."

Jessie took another tentative step forward, worried at how the cop jerked his pistol around when Haze spoke up. She needed to get the situation under control right away. "If we get another quake, even a tremor, Johnny is gonna be flattened. Misha's already dead." Her voice, strong at first, faded when the thought of Misha crawled through her head. She'd already lost him…she didn't want to talk about the two upstairs.

"Lost one in there?" His hard eyes seemed to lighten up and shoulders relax.

Jessie nodded. "Maybe three; I don't know what happened to the two that were upstairs." She'd wanted to say "my boyfriend", but that didn't seem to sit well in her mouth now; nothing did other than "hurry the fuck up and help us", but that wouldn't come forward either.

The cops exchanged glances and guns returned to holsters. "Okay. Rook, go see what we've got in the trunk," said the black-haired cop with the US Marine-issue haircut. Then back to Jessie: "No point in calling for a fire truck; they're already all over the city on calls. We'll get him out. Johnny, you say?" He tried on a smile like it was a first time for him, and he took a few steps forward. "I'm Officer Middleton, Mike Middleton. And that's Officer Rodriguez. We're gonna help."

Jessie nodded, then turned to Haze, and seeing him still kneeling there with his hands up, she reached over and touched him, pushing his arms down. They fell with a little protest, as if he wasn't ready to believe he wasn't going off to jail or getting shot, and then he just looked at her and stood up. "It's cool," she said. "They're going to help us." Or at least she hoped they would.

Damien came up behind her, dusting off his knees, then slipped around the side, keeping Jessie between himself and the policeman. "In our hood, sister, the cops don't come round to help. They come round to put niggas in jail."

Jessie exchanged glances with him, then her eyes found Haze's again, and he nodded. "I guess it's a little different over here in Fells."

"I guess." Damien shrugged.

"Sorry."

"Nothing to be sorry about, shorty. But I think we'll leave that knife right where he dropped it, a'ight." He smirked when he said it.

"Gotcha. Well, thanks for trying anyway. If you don't mind hanging out a few minutes while we do this rescue, I'd appreciate it."

"He'd appreciate your number," said Damien, leaning in and waggling his caterpillar-like brows at Jessie.

Haze rolled his eyes. "D, I'd appreciate it if you'd go back in and let Johnny know that we're about to kick this party off."

"Me? Fuck. A'ight, but I ain't staying in there. If that roof comes down, you ain't dragging my dead ass outta there later, yo. Got that?"

He disappeared through the kitchen door, then Jessie turned back, finding the other cop, Rodriquez, coming up with what looked like a crowbar in one hand and the handle from a tire jack in the other. "It's all I could find, Mike. We don't exactly have demo gear in the car."

Mike nodded. "It'll have to do, Rook. This brick is pretty old, maybe even just a single layer, and it's been shifting in the quakes, so we might be able to get through it quickly." He took the crowbar from his partner and stepped forward, looking at the wall. "Where we talking? Got a reference point for me?"

Haze stepped up and pointed. "Somewhere here, I figure, is the middle of those double doors. They were sealed up then bricked over. I was gonna try and get through with that knife, maybe get a few bricks lose, and then hopefully they all come out a few at a time."

"Okay, let's get to it then. You're over here, Rook." Officer Rodriguez nodded and pushed through the others behind Mike just as the Earth shuddered and did a few jumping jacks, sending them slamming into the bricks.

Jessie screamed when she felt the ground drop out from under her feet. Then it thrust up again like an uppercut, slamming her jaw shut and jarring her spine. Arms flailing, she crashed against the asphalt, then flipped as the ground rolled, giving no indication it would end its deadly calisthenics. She scrambled on all fours, trying desperately to stay in contact with the parking lot, her head whipping about. She could see Haze; he mirrored her labored crawling as the building behind her, the place she called home, groaned under the onslaught. Suddenly the ground dropped out from under her, and she found herself tumbling to the blacktop again when it settled, cracks forming like spiderwebs in every direction.

Haze tumbled into her, the weight of his body another shock to her system, but a comfort, too. She latched onto his arm, hoping his strength would stop the world from shaking her to pieces, and maybe it would get them both out of this alive. But there was no reprieve, and her mouth opened and screamed again of its own accord. Not even her body was under her control now as the blacktop flipped them like hotcakes.

The ground shifted hard again, bucked them into the air like a wild stallion, then dropped another dozen feet as if a giant sinkhole was opening around them. Jessie hit the ground and saw stars, her cheek burning from the impact, her eyes momentarily registering the broadside of One-Eyed Mike's just as the bricks they were about to breach exploded.

Silence. Darkness. Rush of air.

Jessie blinked, her ears ringing, her vision blurry. For a moment she wondered where she was. It'd been another wild night - too much drinking, if there was such a concept, not enough food, and then Rick's whiskey dick until she'd forgotten what day it was. It always left her a little light-headed, a little dazed and confused like she was now. All she had to do was roll over, her head splitting open from the rum punches and her body sore in the usual places.

She smiled to herself, but her face didn't follow the lead. It was hot and it hurt, and it was simply not up for the task. Then Jessie's eyes blinked into focus, and she saw the smoldering piece of wood next to her shoulder. The world had turned sideways, or was it her that was all wrong? Then the memory of the explosion played back in her head in full HD as if she'd missed it the first time around and she screamed.

"Rick!" She would have bolted up, if she'd been able, but the effort required for that kind of hurried movement was more than she could muster. Instead, it was a long, tortuous series of twists, shards of pain stabbing through her skull and her chest, until she was on her hands and knees, and only then did she see what was left of her home, smell the charred wood.

From front to back there was still some of the place remaining, but a sizeable chunk in the middle was gone, blown into pieces all around her. Bits of wood and plaster smoldered nearby, and chunks of blackened brick littered the parking lot like moon rocks. One-Eyed Mikes was mortally wounded, folded in on itself, and that death, amongst others, was reflected in the tears streaming down her burning cheeks.

"Rick."

"I thought his name was Johnny." Haze sat up a few feet from her, his words coming between fits of coughing. He brushed some debris out of his hair, wiped his face with his hand and winced. His forehead, and now his hand, was smeared with blood.

"Yes, but Rick was in there, too, on the second floor. He was..." The last of those words was drowned out in a great moan as the front of Mike's shivered and collapsed, flattening like a fallen house of cards. Jessie watched it go, unable to look away or even utter another sound. All she could hear was her own labored breathing and the ground beneath them trembling again.

"D! Damien!" Haze pushed up, groaning as he did it. "He went in. We sent him in there." Haze climbed to his feet, stumbled forward, coughing, wiping his face again. "D!"

"Here." The voice seemed to come from far away, and then a pile of rubble and what had once been a bush planted in the ground shifted. Haze hobbled over and reached down, pulling on the arm that came up to greet him. He drug a dust-covered body to its feet, and then Damien doubled over in a fit of coughing and choking.

Jessie watched them through the steady drizzle, or was it tears burning her cheeks? She couldn't look back at the building again, and instead she focused on the only two people in her shrinking world.

"You okay, dog? What happened?"

"Damn, Haze," said Damien between hacks, stumbling forward now away from what was left of the tavern. "Don't know. Went in, told that guy what we was doing, left him with old girl's lighter because he said he didn't wanna stand there in the dark no more, then I come out and everything ...." He dropped to one knee before he could continue, his hand reaching up to his face, fingers touching his nose gingerly. "Not my fucking day," was all he could say.

"Not nobody's day, dog."

Jessie heard the words and somehow smiled, thankful that there wasn't another person lost to the building, but that smile faded when her eyes drifted left and locked on the collapsed rowhomes the next street over. Between them, a flood of gray-black water sloshed and foamed as it crashed into every break and barrier in its path, but it came on, blasting debris out of the way in a race towards the desolate little parking lot next to what used to be a cozy little tavern. Their ship was about to set sail, maybe for the last time.

"Haze!"

He spun back and then turned to follow her pointing finger. "Fuck. Grab your pack and let's go. We didn't bring a boat. D, gotta jet now, dog."

Jessie gritted her teeth and took a few steps toward her own pack - her world was there now. Whatever she'd hoped to accomplish was gone; whoever she'd hoped to save was gone. Misha gone. Johnny gone. Rick and Roxie gone, too. All that was left was to get away. She lumbered after Damien and grabbed her backpack, ignoring the blackened brick and exposed beams on her right. They'd do what they could for Johnny and Misha and Rick and Roxie afterward - say some words and maybe even…maybe even forgive, but for now they had to leave them. There was nothing else.

Spinning round, Jessie's eyes found Officer Mike on his back, his head twisted at a gruesome angle, neck bloodied and broken. But Officer Rodriguez was moving, climbing to his feet. He was wobbly, but he was alive, Haze already crossing the debris field to help him up. And then Damien was shoving her forward, his hand on her arm, squeezing maybe a little too hard. She moved, letting him propel her, but before she could take a half dozen steps, a voice froze her in her tracks.

"Jessie. Baby, I thought you were dead."

She turned and her knees threatened to buckle as Rick slid through a gap in the back fence, all smiles and torn shirt and black stains covering his chest.

"You? How? I thought…"

"Back fire escape from the bathroom. Before we -."

But Damien cut him off. "Run, Haze! Harbor's coming!"

Jessie just stared, not sure what to do or say, ignoring the hand dragging her backwards. Then another figure pushed through the hole in the fence and waved. "You left me!" Roxie snarled and barreled into Rick, her arms whipping around him in a deathlock. "But I'm here now." He seemed not to notice, but he didn't move away from the contact. Instead, he stood there, seemingly unaware of where things stood and unsure of the frown that stole over Jessie's face.

"We gotta go." It was Damien, his voice close in her ear, his hand gripping her arm. "Who's that?"

"Don't worry about it," she muttered, pointing at the oncoming water. "Worry about that!" Then she turned and ran.

Jessie scanned the street as they lumbered out onto the cobblestones. The police cars were still huddled in the middle of Bond Street about half a block down, two of the cops there and a few residents milling about. Haze led the way there, pulling Officer

Rodriguez along behind him. The cop looked to be the worst for wear out of them all. He was limping badly, and his shirt and pants were shredded in the front, replaced with splotches of reddened skin. Haze was supporting him under one arm, and Jessie took up station on the other side, trying to help them forward. None of them was in any condition to run, so a fast zombie shamble would have to do.

The other two cops came forward as soon as they saw their man.

"Flaco, you alright, hombre?"

He mumbled something, but Haze was faster on the draw. "There was an explosion, and he's hurt, but your other officer, Mike - he's dead. Back there by that bar."

The cop looked at him as if he'd heard the report wrong, then his eyes were focused on Rodriquez. "Where's Mike, Flaco?"

"He told ya, Bill. Dead. Wall exploded in that last quake, and he got it worse than me."

"And now the harbor's flooding in," Jessie blurted out just as she heard the first splash underfoot, saw the cobblestones awash in murky water. "Gotta get outta here. Can you drive us out?" She and Haze stepped back as the other two officers took on their burden.

"We'll look after Flaco here, but you, um -." Bill the Cop looked up and counted the faces that looked back at him. "You five need to keep moving. Get to open ground in case there are more tremors and wait for assistance. We'll have more personnel coming to help with quake victims as soon as possible, but we have to stick around here and help out people who are trapped or hurt."

"Whoa! You fucking kidding me, dog?" Damien chimed in from the back row, where he stayed.

"I got orders."

"Fuck your orders. We already handled that earthquake. We need rescued from a flood."

"What flood?"

"That fucking flood," said Jessie, pointing as the first wave swept into the street and foamed up around the mostly upright live oaks still lining the sidewalks. "And what the hell is that?"

The water was pooling fast, swirling in the hollows of the warped pavement, only it wasn't just water that was moving back by the old bar. There was something else, something blue-black like a cloud's shadow dancing across the wet concrete, and when it came forward, swiveling on eight legs, massive claws in the air, the only thing Jessie could hear was her scream.

7

IT MOVED SO FAST, THEY barely had a chance to get around the cop cars before it was barreling into them, metal screeching, claws snapping, then what could only be the warbling wail of the crabby monstrosity as bullets thudded into its hardened shell.

It was no joke. It was real, and Haze had seen it when they'd left the construction site - or he'd thought he had. That was crazy talk, wasn't it? He'd looked back and seen a crab this size and color rising from the ooze of the shattered pavement, mud and debris sliding off its shell as water from the harbor pooled around its spindly legs. But he'd shrugged it off, not said a word to Damien. He didn't wanna hear about the "giant crab" for the rest of his life. The boys on the block were merciless, and D would tell them all the moment he hit the corner. So, he'd dropped it and hadn't looked back. Enough bullshit had happened for one day, and he'd crashed against the asphalt more than a few times, hard hat tumbling away like a broken helmet, thanks to the tremors. He'd imagined it, a concussion maybe, and then they'd scampered over the low berm and crossed the street, leaving that delusion and the rising water behind.

But this was real, at least Haze was pretty sure it was, and real or not, they needed to get the fuck up outta there.

"Get behind us now!" Bill screamed between shots, waving his free hand. His partner stepped into formation beside him, police-issue automatic up and firing almost point-blank range as one of the massive claws crushed the hood of the patrol car. The metal screamed and folded. The front tires blew out with its next blow, and the windshield shattered next.

Haze reached out to pull Jessie and Damien back away from the car as it skidded under the heavy-weight assault of the gigantic crustacean, but they didn't need any prodding. They hurried around to the back of the second police car and gaped with the others. It seemed like a safe distance if that was even possible. From there they watched the Battle of Bond Street.

The whole scene was surreal at best. The official food of Baltimore was standing not ten yards away taller than the vehicle it was currently shredding with its massive claws, and wider, too. Two beady orbs peeked out from the upper shell, which was reddish gray in color in the bleak morning fog. Where was the Old Bay? Where were the hammers and the little forks? Where were the Natty Bohs? And why was dinner as big as an SUV and more dangerous than any character from The Wire?

Damien popped Haze with an elbow and motioned to the pistol he had in his waistband, but Haze shook him off and leaned in. "Not now, not here. Cops are still cops, D, even when..." He let it go, unsure of what to say and unable to look away.

"Where yours? The one I gave you?"

Haze shook his head. "Dropped it somewhere back there. Don't know where. I didn't think I'd be needing it, so I didn't worry about it."

"Yo, that shit cost me; guns ain't free."

Haze ignored him, watching the cops and crab slog it out, mano a .... whatever. He felt a thrill when he saw the monster's movements slow, the bullets penetrating its shell one after the other. The car was now a wreck, both the hood and roof crushed, and the normal paint job was smeared with the bluish fluid that oozed from the creature's wounds. It looked like it'd be over in a few moments. Then suddenly the thing seemed to shift, whether off balance or simply from understanding the situation, and it lurched to the left around the crumpled hood of the Crown Vic with a speed that sent everyone reeling. But it found its prey within reach.

Bill screamed as the massive claw closed in and cleaved him in two, his finger still on the trigger as a shot rang out when his torso splashed into the bloody water below. The other officer scrambled backwards but found his way blocked by the other squad car, his gun empty, the click-click of the useless weapon nearly drowned out by the snapping of the creature's claws. "Fuck you!" he bellowed and threw the revolver at the monster just before he whirled and tried to flip over the hood of the car. Too late, a giant, blood-stained claw flattened him against the hood, and he fell still.

"My turn, Haze!" It was Damien at his shoulder, his own 9mm coming up to fire, but before he could even squeeze off a shot, Flaco shambled around the hood of the second car, shotgun aimed and firing. He shuddered with each shot, limping forward and trying to steady himself against the bulk of the vehicle, each step in sync with the shotgun's thunder until they were face-to-face, cop versus crustacean. Flaco pressed the barrel of the shotgun to the crab's shell, pulled the trigger one last time. Blue-green goo splattered across his face and torn shirt, then he fell back against the broken squad car, weapon still aimed and ready as the creature's legs buckled and it collapsed with a splash.

"Fuck yeah!" Rick's voice rang out over the silenced crowd, and he rushed around the car with Roxie in tow to congratulate Flaco. The officer was leaning against the hood of his squad car, the shotgun aimed at the ground but still at the ready. He nodded at whatever words Rick passed on and pushed through them as he clapped him on the back.

"Ew! He's covered in that thing's goop," said Roxie, dancing away from the cop, then Rick. "Don't you dare touch me with that hand until you wash it."

Haze rolled his eyes as the two turned to stare at the dead thing in the street. He shrugged and turned his attention to Flaco, met him near the trunk. "Now what, Flaco? Get you to the hospital? You alright?"

"That was some crazy shit, dog," said Damien, who hovered behind Haze as if he was afraid to get closer to the massive dead crustacean.

Flaco nodded, his eyes downcast. "We're not going to get any help right now. We're on our own."

"We need a car," said Rick, apparently over his fascination with the dead monster.

"I'm coming, too," said Roxie. "Nobody's leaving me here in this shit. Don't forget me, baby." She sidled up to Rick, wrapping her meaty arms around him, eyes daring anyone to say otherwise.

Haze ignored them. "What do we do with your, um, you know." He pointed back at the fallen, unsure of what to say. What could they do? They couldn't just leave the officers who'd saved them from the crab to float away in the flood, could they? Besides, they weren't a threat anymore; no one would be looking for the payroll robbers now.

"Yo no se." Flaco sighed, his eyes still aimed at his shoes like the shotgun. "Don't know. Only been on the force nine months. They don't train us for this shit, man."

Haze nodded. "Yeah, no shit." The two looked at each other, and Haze realized at that moment that he was the quarterback for this team now, and they were waiting for someone to call a play. He looked past the beat-up cop to the two extras they'd picked up at the collapsed bar. Behind him stood Damien and Jessie, both just standing, waiting. Not much of a team, but he'd had worse, especially in his freshman year on the JV squad.

For a moment, the world stood still and waited, as if a big decision moment was at hand. Water sloshed around their feet and splashed up against the back fender of the destroyed Crown Vic. The shotgun hung limply in Flaco's grip, and his breathing was uneven. The rain came down, still a drizzle, but he could feel the cool drops fall across his hot face. A siren shrieked in the distance, and Haze blinked and stepped back, the field coming into view. It was time to call the play. "We ain't got time for this. We gotta jet. Everybody, we can't drive out. Gotta hoof it, so let's go. Water's coming in fast."

He looked up and found all eyes on him. Jessie nodded. Flaco just blinked. Roxie's face was twisted up, her mouth opening. "Who put you in charge?" Rick's face reflected hers, but before he could say a word, Haze was already replying.

"No one. I'm just leaving with my boy here, and Flaco." He hesitated, turning to Jessie.

"And me. I'm coming with." She looked right back at him, ignoring the grunt from the back row.

"Then let's go."

"Wait. Hold up. I gotta get this shit on video," said Damien, suddenly animated. He fished around in his pocket and produced his cell phone. "Nobody's gonna believe it. Can't just leave it."

"Not now, dog," said Haze, yanking on Damien's shoulder strap, but he pulled free and sloshed forward. "D, let's go. The water. Jessie?"

"We need a car," she said and half-nodded toward the black and white they stood behind.

"I don't think -," but those were the only words out of Haze's mouth as he looked past Damien still intent on a picture and now trying to maneuver himself into position to get a selfie with the dead creature.

"Nobody's gonna believe this shit, yo. Gotta do it; throw this shit up on Instagram. Hash tag: crabcake." He laughed at his own joke.

"You mean crabquake," said Roxie, following up. "Gonna message me those pics, right?"

But Haze wasn't really listening; he was moving around the nearest car to get a better view.

"What is it?" Jessie turned when she saw the look on his face.

"More of those fuckers," he said, "and they brought the whole family."

Suddenly two more crabs emerged from the parking lot behind One-Eyed Mikes, both as big as the one they'd just taken down. They skittered forward slowly, shifting from side to side on their multi-jointed legs as if they were bobbing and weaving in preparation for a fight. Heavy claws that were now known to do some damage moved in sync with the crabs' dance like deadly boxing gloves. All around their legs, the water seethed as smaller crabs, some miniscule greenish ones floating on the incoming tide, some big as cats or even large dogs swooping in with the waves, gathered like an army of miniature minions, cannon fodder for what battle would come.

"And Mrs. Swaslowski."

"What?" Haze dropped his gaze and focused down Jessie's line of sight, blinking against the rain that was picking up. Her finger pointed out the predicament.

Opposite the fallen bar, in front of the line of crumbling rowhomes, an old woman stood up to her knees in water, the bottom of her sky-blue robe caught up in one hand to keep it dry while the other hand held a tiny flip phone. She was facing what was once her home, shouting into the receiver in what must have been Polish, completely oblivious to the normally dine-in/carry out danger only a dozen yards away.

"We gotta get her out of there," mumbled Jessie, and before Haze could react, she was off, splashing forward.

"Wait. Fuck! Jessie, we can't." Haze stood there, his arm out impotently reaching for her again, but she ignored him, pushing past the cop cars and moving quickly over to what was once the sidewalk on the east side of Bond Street, keeping the trees between herself and the crabs. "Fuck." What was she doing? Being a hero? And yet, it was a little old lady that she knew, and wouldn't he, shouldn't he be doing what she was doing? The cop wasn't going to do it. Damien was still snapping pictures, and the other two - they were useless.

"Jessie!" It was Rick now calling after her, but she ignored him, as well. His head swiveled, first towards Jessie, then back to Haze, and finally his gaze rested on Roxie, who stood behind him, hands on her hips. "I should go after her," was all he could muster before Haze brushed past, his broad shoulder connecting with Rick's, spinning him around and almost knocking him over.

Haze snatched the shotgun from Flaco's hands and said, "I'll bring it right back, Flaco. I got some business. You get us ready to move; take whatever we can carry."

Eyes shifting from predator to prey, or at least that's how he saw it, Haze moved up Bond Street a dozen yards behind Jessie. It was only about a half block up to the old woman, Mrs. What's-It-Ski's - he hadn't caught the name exactly, but it was like walking uphill in the snow. The water was still rising, now nearly mid-calf, and Haze didn't want to splash or make any more noise than he had to. There was no telling what would trigger an attack - were the crabs sensitive to movement? Were they attuned to attack things that made noise like he'd heard about in some zombie flicks? Zombies went for loud sounds. Maybe crabs operated the same way; that is, giant, fucking mutant crabs - wherever the hell they came from. There was no way to know. There was only the game plan: grab the old lady and get the hell outta there.

"Fucking D," he grumbled under his breath. "All this shit's his fault." The dumbass was probably still trying to get a good picture of the dead crab, but then again, Haze knew, he wouldn't have been any help. Damien still liked to hold his pistol sideways like he'd seen in one of those old Ice Cube flicks, where everybody's a gangbanger. Or maybe that was a video. What mattered now was that he was out of the way and wouldn't cause any problems. He was better off with Jessie.

Then he looked up, and the crabs were moving, Mrs. Blue-Robe-ski was waving her arms and yelling into the phone, and Jessie was screaming and running.

Haze started running, too, but he could already tell he was going to be too late. The crabs were going to slice and dice that old woman before she could even say "Charm City", and then he'd have to worry about getting Jessie out of there. He clutched the shotgun, hoping it still had shells in it.

Before he'd taken ten steps, the crabs descended on the old woman. She spun around from the sound of the splashing and yelled once more into the phone before she screamed at the nearest crab. It warbled, but hesitated, apparently unprepared for the verbal onslaught, but it took only a moment for the eardrum shattering screech to end, and the crab moved in. A few tiny steps from the eight legs got the creature within striking distance, its mottled claw up for a smash rather than a grab, but the helpless little old lady reached out her arm and yelled, "Eat pepper, crabby!"

She let out a blood-curdling scream as she loosed a stream of yellowish liquid from the tiny cannister in her palm, and the crab screamed in response, stopping dead in its tracks, and then lurching backwards, crashing into the second monster. It stumbled, tumbled to the ground, claws flailing, legs wobbling until they failed, and its bottom shell hit the water with a pathetic sploosh just as Jessie arrived.

Haze was only a few steps behind, shotgun coming up. "Go! Go!" he said, and he checked the safety and the action in the seconds before the second crab could orient around the first and move in. He heard more than saw the two women moving behind him, his whole focus on what was rushing him with a speed that rivaled anything he'd seen in a high school middle linebacker, and infinitely heavier. "Aim and shoot," he muttered, pressing the butt of the pump action Mossberg to his shoulder, and he fired.

The sound, as much as the kick, shook him, spinning Haze around and throwing him on his face into the water. He coughed and sputtered, trying to get his bearings, trying to keep his head above water that tasted like what cat piss mixed with month-old milk might taste like, at least that's what floated through his mind when he tried to spit it out. He scrambled on hands and knees, fingers still locked on the shotgun, and came up, head spinning, finding the second crab ambling one way then another, as if it was disoriented. The first was still floundering in the water, but it looked like it was getting itself together.

That was enough time for Haze, and he turned and bolted, pulling his bag back up on his shoulder and cradling the shotgun. There was no reason to hang around; he couldn't even be sure if he had another shot. And Jessie and the old lady were almost back to the police cars now. The rest of the crew there were waving her on, now him, like parents at a track meet. He didn't need to be told twice.

He ran.

Back at the cop cars, they were ready to go. Jessie met Haze when he stopped, out of breath and unprepared when she smiled as she wrapped her arms around him. She let go quickly and stepped back, her eyes avoiding his for a moment. "Thanks for coming to get us."

"No problem. You did something brave. I couldn't let you go by yourself."

She nodded, and this time her eyes met his.

"Sorry, I'm all wet," he said, looking down at himself, suddenly self-conscious. "And I stink now."

"You kinda do," said Jessie, wrinkling her nose. Then she giggled.

"Gonna need some new clothes soon."

"And about a million wet wipes. What's in the bag? After work clothes?" She indicated the coveralls he was still wearing.

Haze swallowed, wiped the greasy water from his face. "No, not really. Are we ready to go?" He looked past her, suddenly very aware of the black bag over his shoulder and what other questions she might have.

"Yeah," said Flaco, stepping up. "Hurry before those things get moving again." He pointed down the street, where the crabs seemed to be gathering themselves. "You must have shot it in the face or something, huh?"

Haze shrugged. "What did that old lady have? Whatever it was, that shit worked."

"Pepper spray," said Jessie, her arm around Mrs. Swaslowski's shoulders. The woman looked more perturbed than afraid as she fingered the keyboard on her cell.

"I was in the middle of the call," she muttered, not looking up.

Haze shrugged, looked to Flaco, but he just shook his head. "Where to?"

"This way," said Jessie, and she moved out, hand-in-hand with the little old lady, around the corner and down Lancaster Street. "We need to get to high ground, somewhere the flood and the crabs, if there are more of them, can't get us."

Everyone followed, feet splashing, legs sloshing through green-black harbor water down the middle of another narrow, historic lane paved with cobblestones they couldn't see anymore. They weaved around the obstacle course that consisted primarily of small cars turned every which way and a couple of houses that hadn't been as sturdy as others. The street was eerily deserted, only the sounds of their splashing and breathing evidence that there was any life in the historic neighborhood. The other residents they'd seen earlier were already long gone, making Haze wonder if there was some kind of storm shelter or anti-crab sanctuary nearby that he didn't know about.

At the end of the block, they found themselves in Broadway Square, an open space bounded by bars and restaurants on three sides, the Inner Harbor on the other. It was the centerpiece of the historic neighborhood, only now it looked like a war zone, complete with a helicopter hovering over the square, both doors open, revealing a pair of helmeted heads. People were everywhere, sitting on cars, sloshing through the knee-high water to wherever. It was a typical Saturday night, only it wasn't a weekend night, and the square was quickly filling with water.

"Rescue?" It was Roxie's shrill squeak that broke the silence. "It could rescue us!" She screamed and waved.

Everyone was looking, Damien and Roxie yelling up at the chopper as it circled and slid sideways to the far side of the square. It slowed and began to hover just over the top of the buildings there, three story structures like old rowhomes, some sporting second and third floor apartments over ground floor retail space. And then like a mindless herd, they all began to run.

"Definitely a rescue," shouted Rick, pointing. There were maybe a dozen people on the roof at the southeast corner of the square. "There, on top of Woody's. Run!" He was out in front before he'd even finished yelling, pulling Roxie behind him, and everyone followed.

Haze brought up the rear, glancing left and right for signs of trouble, the Mossberg at the ready. What they'd left behind was gone, and what was in front of them was a rescue - there was no going back. Finally, they'd be the hell out of this bullshit, and he'd have the seed money and even felt a little like a hero, odd as that was. He was protecting this little group of misfits, among them a cop that Jessie was helping limp along. He watched her support a man she didn't know at all, surprised at what he'd seen in her. He'd been even more surprised at the hug, but that was nothing, he was sure. Just a show of gratitude. There was definitely something between her and the other dude in the group, even though he was holding hands with the thick chick.

It didn't matter. He'd be gone soon - gone from the Charm City and on to culinary school somewhere where it was warmer, maybe Florida, and Baltimore's giant crabs and even bigger crime and poverty problems would be far behind. Not to mention the West Side, the hood rats, and even D. He needed to let it all go.

Flaco didn't say a word when Rick kicked at a plain white door on the side of an ice cream shop. Behind it a flight of stairs led up to the third floor. They scrambled up the long line of steps, even with Flaco's limp, and burst into what turned out to be Woody's, a sort of Caribbean-themed bar that overlooked the Broadway Pier, what was left of it, and the encroaching harbor. Then they were winding around to another even narrower flight of steps that led to the roof, where they stopped and watched the helicopter lift away, its cabin brimming with relieved faces.

"Fuck," said Damien. "This not how I planned to spend my Friday."

8

THE WHOP-WHOP OF THE helicopter's rotors faded away, and Jessie wiped a tear from her cheek as she led the way back down to the bar. No one would see it, and that was for the best. She could already hear Rick's voice behind her but directed at Roxie, who was bawling like a banshee and flooding the narrow stairwell with sobbing profanity. No, he wouldn't see her cry. She'd already shed too many of her tears on him. Never again.

Back on the third floor, the little tiki bar filled the entirety of the narrow space before them, now more a collection of clutter with an underlying scent of extra strength cleaner. Woody's was known for its overly late nights and overabundance of spilled drinks. How many times had she sat up here in the Crow's Nest, as she and Rick had called it, leaning on the white rails, watching the drunken catastrophe below, the vomitrocity committed against Fells Point every weekend night? A drunk girl with impossibly high heels trying to negotiate the cobblestones? A posse of frat boys on a bar crawl trying to make it from one end of Thames Street to the other without a trip to the ER? Sheila and Misty would turn out the lights and send everyone home, everyone except their favorites, who would "man the rails" with Rum Runners in hand and watch the old neighborhood bar scene go completely into the shitter. Fells Point after-hours: it was people watching at its best.

But now the scenery had changed, and the Rum Runners were a thing of the past, if what she'd seen so far was any indication. Jessie collapsed into the first upright chair she came to, setting her backpack on the table and staring out through the cracked plexiglass at what was once a quaint little scene, now more like the scene of a crime.

"Dios mio," said Flaco, groaning with each breath as Haze lowered him into a seat nearby then set the Mossberg on the table, a reminder of what was waiting out there for them.

Jessie stared at the shotgun for a moment, distracted, then her eyes went to the injured cop, then to Haze standing behind him. He stared out through the broken set of plastic shutters and peeled off the dirty, soaked coveralls, revealing a maroon t-shirt that read "Bolts" and "7" across the back and a pair of black jeans that fit, she realized, exactly like they were supposed to. He dropped the wet clothing at his feet next to the black bag and stretched while she inhaled the scene, watching the lines in his arms and shoulders flow like an impromptu ballet. An athlete, she thought. Or a dancer.

"Yeah, what the fuck happened?" Haze's voice drifted out over the advancing water, caught in a morning breeze and whispered away. He turned back, shaking his head, and locked eyes with Jessie before she could drop her gaze.

She swallowed, her eyes suddenly in her lap, feeling a little rush of fear, butterflies. "I dunno."

"The pier is pretty much gone. That new restaurant, the Mexican one, whatever it was called, used to be an oyster place - it's flat as a pancake and half underwater. I never even went there once. You?"

"Yeah," she said, looking up, trying to look past him to the place he'd mentioned, but he was staring at her, and she couldn't see anything past him. "It was okay. The food, that is. The margaritas were all mix - lazy bartenders."

Someone laughed behind them, and the spell was broken when Haze looked up at the bar. "Um, drink anyone? I could use one."

"Any tequila back there?" Flaco attempted a smile, but he couldn't manage it. Just twisting in the chair made him wince and cough.

"Tequila?" Old bartending habits kicked in, and Jessie needed to get moving and breathe.

Haze nodded, and Jessie spun out of her chair. "I'll have a look. Meanwhile, didn't we bring a first aid kit with us from the squad car?" See caught Haze's eye. "Can you take a look at him; clean him up a little?"

He nodded, offered her up a smile. "Gotcha."

She offered him a feeble smile back, the little flutter filling her belly, and she turned to the bar. There was certainly no time for that, no matter how pretty he was. No matter how his smile reached up into his eyes. No time for that.

A dozen steps turned that flutter into fire when she found Rick at the bar, a bottle of Parrot Bay in his left hand, a sizeable piece of ass in his right. She frowned, watched his fingers groping. Don't care, she told herself. Haze was watching, wasn't he?

Damien was behind the bar, too, searching through the few cabinets there. And Roxie. She was sitting tight, as usual, on a bar stool, her too short, formerly white shorts smudged and soaked through in all the wrong places, and her big fat ass molding into the fingers that gripped it. Her eyes were fixed on the drink in her hand, her sobs gone now as she smiled into a plastic cup of something that would surely take the edge off. Rick was good like that. He'd always been good like that.

Jessie sighed, shook her head. "Jesus, I need a drink." The bottle of Parrot Bay looked enticing as all fuck. And when in Rome...

"Yeah, they'll come back and get us in a jiffy, baby," said Rick, his eyes on the prize. He blinked and threw Jessie a grin when she approached, but it was forced, too toothy, the "I didn't do nothing, baby" smile that smelled of forthcoming confessions, tears and the shattering of a favorite beer stein against a wall.

"Better bring two choppers to fit us all in." Damien turned around with a bottle of Jose Cuervo in hand and a bunch of shot glasses that spilled out of his big paw all over the bar. "We be right fucked up by then, ready to get our rescue on and get to partying. Hey now!" He grinned from ear to ear, a glint of silver on the right side of his mouth, his eyes devouring the huge tracts of land before him. It was like feeding time, and Roxie was the zebra.

She was already the winner of the Friday morning wet t-shirt contest, and she knew it. No way she'd accidentally left her bra in the apartment. "You think? Oh awesome!" Roxie giggled and jiggled, and Damien leaned in a little closer, practically drooling, the shot glasses forgotten.

"Who wants a little Jose?" said Damien as Jessie sidled up to the bar. He grinned at her, and Jessie threw him a reply smile laced with cold fire. He withered, his gaze lingering only a moment. Then she reached out and snatched the bottle right out of his hand. "Table six does."

"The fuck?" was the only thing she heard as she spun away with a few plastic cups in hand. She dropped them on their own table and flicked off the top of the bottle under the watchful and appreciative eyes of the two men seated there. Haze was in the process of rooting through the small first aid kit they'd brought along, but he stopped long enough to watch a professional at work, giving her a long look as if maybe he could read her, could understand the storm that was brewing inside.

"Drinks on the house, boys." Jessie poured with the casual precision of a pro, then gathered up her cup and hoisted it in the air. "To survival and a little Old Bay revenge in our future."

"Give me a mallet and bib," said Flaco, coughing again, "and we're in business, cabrón."

"You got it down already. From around here?"

"San Antonio. They needed Spanish-speaking officers up here for all these Latinos, so I moved and signed up."

"Welcome to the Charm City," said Jessie and handed Haze his cup.

"Real fucking charming," he said and raised his glass.

They all laughed at that and tipped their cups back. The room temperature tequila went back with a welcome bite, a little 'happy to be alive' reminder. Jessie's eyes lingered on Haze a moment, then strayed back to Flaco, to the blood on his face, the way his eyes looked heavy as the cup came away from his lips. He needed a little pain killer, so she poured another round and nodded at the first aid kit.

"We'll need some sanitary wipes to clean up the cuts," said Jessie. "No telling what's in that water, but we wanna cut off any infections at the pass, if we can. Then there's some bandages and tape. Should be easy to handle, but I'll be back in a sec, and I can help. K?"

Flaco looked up from the kit to his triage nurse. "You an EMT or something? Nurse?"

She shook her head. "Bartender, but I watch a lot of that medical TV channel and we get lots of after-hours docs and nurses at Mike's for drinks and dinner. You pick up a few things. Comes in handy when people have had a little too much to drink."

"Regular girl scout," said Haze as he pulled out a packet of sanitary wipes and ripped it open.

"They've got the best cookies," Jessie said and flushed, suddenly aware of what she'd said. "Now, I'm gonna check on the rest of our passengers and spread the Jose love. I'll be back."

Haze looked like he could handle his part of the deal, so Jessie was going to work hers, and get the hell away from that table as fast as possible before she said something else stupid.

As a professional social butterfly, she couldn't resist the urge to check on the others, but she kept her gaze inside the broken plexiglass that lined two walls. She didn't want to see what was out there until she had to. There were things here that might need tending to, and that was something she could manage. Their little group of misfits wasn't the only thing left behind up on that rooftop. There'd been a handful of people stranded when the chopper lifted off, full and slow like a predator after the kill. She'd heard the screams of those left behind, the curses and threats, and she'd heard their quiet murmurs, their guarded growls as they'd flooded in behind her and filled up the chairs, spreading their whole lives out on cheap plastic tables.

The room reeked of harbor water, like the B.O. of a thousand dead fish, and it looked like the last refuge of Noah's Ark rejects. She pressed through a small crowd of sad-looking faces and handed out plastic cups and shots. Some took them; others poked at their phones, trying to get a message out. Still others just stood there and stared through her like zombies. Past them, a couple holding hands at one of the corner tables and whispering to themselves clammed up when Jessie stopped. Both were barefoot and wore little more than t-shirts and shorts, as if they'd had just enough time to throw something on and get outdoors. When she lifted the bottle their way in a silent offering, the guy shook his head. His wife, the ring on her finger gleaming through the gloom like a lighthouse, didn't even look up. Her head hung down, her face masked by a nest of wet brown hair. "We have a first aid kit over at that table with my friend and the cop if you need anything." The guy nodded and stroked his wife's hand, his fingers lingering over her massive rock.

Two older guys in running gear looked up from their table, the lines in their faces crisscrossing in jagged, age-engraved patterns. But their eyes were bright, and they smiled when she pushed through to them. "Is there a movie on this flight, stewardess?" offered one of them, his voice rough and scratchy like he'd gargled with the broken glass underfoot.

"No, but there's free booze at the bar and the seatbelt light is off."

"Any of that left?" Glass-Voice indicated the bottle of Jose Cuervo Jessie was still carrying.

She smiled her best "I like big tips" smile and set two plastic cups on the table and poured long and deep. "It's all-you-can-drink today, boys. Thanks for flying Jessie Air."

"Pleasure's all ours," said Glass-Voice's friend, peeking out from under a raggedy Orioles ballcap. "I'm Marty; this is Mike. We're in home renovations and real estate."

"And tequila." Marty nodded.

"Nice to meet you. I'm Jessie. I'll be your stewardess and barista all day today, or until our ride comes back for us. Just give me a holler if you need anything, hon." She winked and walked off as they dipped into their cups. Gay men always made for great tips. Especially dirty old gay men with connections and money.

That left Mrs. Swaslowski sitting alone at the last hard plastic table, her flip phone lifted in the air at the end of a long, bony arm. She shifted her gaze when Jessie sat down across from her, a look of grim determination on her face. "No signal. How's it I got no signal?"

"Electricity's out? Towers are down?" Jessie shrugged. "More importantly, are you okay?"

"Oh yeah, hon, I'm okay. Just can't get a signal," she continued, turning back to her phone and raising it up to the sky as if her arm was an antenna. "Was talking to my insurance man, Manny, when that thing came at me. Now can't get him back."

"I'm Jessie, and I'm with those guys," she said, pointing.

"Anna Swaslowski of the Boca Raton Swaslowskis, even if my mama did hustle us off to Indian Town near that god awful lake. Gators and swamps; swamps and gators all day long. Ain't no way to live, hear?" Eyes fixed on the phone; she didn't notice the cup set in front of her.

"Got anyone else to call? Husband? Family? Anyone we should try and contact?"

Mrs. Swaslowski's eyes shifted for a second, falling on Jessie, then they reverted to watching the phone.

"What brought you to Baltimore?"

"Moved up here after a fella some years ago - Bogdan Obuchowski - we called him Barry - after he come home from the war in Korea.

Was back to working for his daddy making sausage. Thought it'd be fine work. Gone some fifteen years now - bless his heart; just sold off one of the shops over yonder on Washington to some sweet boys as was gonna keep up the tradition and the name considering all my children were girls."

"I see." Jessie sat back in the white plastic seat and took a sip of her own plastic cup while Anna seemed intent on aiming her cell at the heavens. "Lived there long? On Bond, right? You live across the street from us."

"Forty-seven years." She said it like there was a prize coming her way. "Right there on Bond Street cross from the bread factory. Worked there a few years, then the dust from all that baking got to my lungs."

"Why didn't you just go into the sausage business, too?"

Anna paused, her arm dropping a bit, and she cast about, her eyes finally coming to rest on the young woman across from her. "Just twixt us girls, didn't much like sausage myself," she muttered, as if she'd been afraid someone would overhear her confession. "Barry, God rest his soul, woulda died outright to hear me say such, hon."

Jessie nodded, took another sip. Polish woman married to a sausage magnate and not a sausage lover - grounds for divorce in Baltimore, if there ever were any. "After you quit working at H&S - it was H&S you worked at, right?" Anna nodded. "What'd you do after that?"

"Axis Chemical, hon. There on the Harbor Point. Worked in the mail room til they shut down. The whole thing polluted, they said. Leaking chemicals all over the harbor and such, but I was never worried."

"Oh yeah? I heard a little something about that, the pollution, before they started building there. All kinds of tests, the EPA, neighborhood groups protesting, chromium."

Anna turned now, her arm dropping and disappearing beneath the long sleeve of her bathrobe. She snapped her flip phone closed and it disappeared into a pocket. She looked left and right again, then leaned onto the table. "Oh, I heard a lot, saw a lot, too. Mail rooms was before computers, ya know? Everything coming in and out through the mail room. Chrome, they said, or something. Chromium did you say? Said it was okay, so what do I know? Then the government said it could kill a fella, this chrome-such. Poison, they said. But ain't that the stuff's on your car bumper? Reckon I don't know. So, they tore it all down and poured the concrete real thick-like, I hear. And they give me a check every month now, and I just watch my shows and water my plants."

"You didn't get sick?"

"Not a bit, hon. Buncha hooey, I thought. Never took a sick day, not once. But hear some workers did. Read some of the mail before we got sent home - big envelopes with red stripes marked 'Urgent' and 'Confidential', but it was government gobbledygook. Nothing I could make no sense of really. Numbers and such. Then they shut it down, and we got our checks and were told to go home. Maybe it did kill some folks. Didn't kill me."

"And maybe now this new company building there is related to these earthquakes? Maybe the chromium turns little crabs into giant killers?" The Jose Cuervo was beginning to feel as good as it tasted, and maybe it was making this old lady's tale sound sensible. Jessie took a bigger sip, wondering at the implications, wondering what this woman might know about what went on there, or if there was anything to it at all. She'd seen the old woman in her bathrobe a thousand times in front of her house watering her potted plants or talking to the neighbors, but they'd never spoken once.

"Oh, can't say, hon. Couldn't say. I know I'm fine. I just need to talk to Manny, get the insurance. That house is all I have," she said as she fished into her pocket again and pulled out the silver flip phone. She opened it and tapped at the screen, then lifted it up into the air, searching the fog.

Jessie stared at her, her thoughts running back to anything and everything she'd heard about the company building on the old Harbor

Point site. The pile drivers had been going for a few weeks. Buildings were up already, but more were coming. But could they have caused the earthquake? Was there poison leaking out into the harbor right now? And is that where those mutated crabs had come from? The chromium? Jessie was sure she'd heard that on the news.

She tipped the bottle again, but this time the cup was left on the table, empty and alone. The glass mouth touched her lips, and she swallowed the burning liquid in hungry gulps, left it on the table when she got up. Whatever Mrs. Swaslowski had said hardly mattered. What mattered was that the harbor was pouring into Fells Point and they were trapped, trapped with something that couldn't exist. And how long before another quake shook the historic district to the ground?

Before she could take a single step, Jessie stopped and turned back to the woman still fixated on her phone, rotating her arm this way and that to try and capture that precocious signal. She'd remembered something she'd wanted to ask - a burning question now. "Mrs. Swaslowski? What's in your other pocket?"

The old woman paused in her efforts and turned to smile at Jessie. "Oh, hon, it's pepper spray. Can't be too careful, you know?"

Then the world shifted again, and the plexi-glass wall fell away, along with the entire corner of the building and the little old woman in the downy blue robe. The silvery phone seemed to hang in the air, and then it vanished, too. A moment later, the floor dropped out from under Jessie.

9

HAZE WHIRLED, HIS REFLEXES kicking in before he even heard Jessie scream, but he missed her outstretched hand, and he tumbled after her.

One moment everything was quiet and fine, Flaco was looking better, his face cleaner but still bruised and torn in places where the brick shrapnel had gashed him. The sanitary wipes were almost gone, but his leg looked better, too, and the gauze there was fresh and clean around his thigh. It would do, Haze thought. It'd have to. All of them would have to go to the hospital anyway, right? He'd heard about the mayor's vision of a swimmable harbor, but that wasn't happening anytime soon; nowadays if you fell in the harbor, you went to the ER - that was the rule. Whatever was in that water wasn't safe, and every one of them had had a heaping helping of it, him more than the others, and the sanitary napkins were long gone before he could get all of it off his face and neck. Now instead of the stench of the harbor, all he could smell was chemical and cleaner.

But that was the least of his worries, right? The water looked dirty enough, but it didn't matter how dirty it was when you drowned in it. And it was flooding in fast and rising by the minute. On top of that they'd run into the weirdest shit imaginable: giant crabs? He shot one in the face, if they even had faces, and he still couldn't believe it. And to make it worse, the whole city had been shaking like his old house back in the day when the Acela Express went by at night.

Haze wanted to sit, put his feet up on the dirty plastic table and have a little more of that tequila. It seemed like the thing to do, but something held him back. The quiet, he thought, had lasted entirely too long, and the booze was flowing, and his boy was acting a fool, trying to talk to the thick chick behind the bar all while the other dude, Rick, was for sure hitting it. His hand was wrist deep in the back of her shorts, grabbing all that fat ass. D didn't have a chance, unless that's how the girl rolled. She didn't seem shy, and you could never tell nowadays. It was fun watching anyway as they pushed shot after shot at her.

But what about Jessie. She'd been unexpected. She'd been chill but brave, too, trying to help her friend in the bar, rushing out to help that little old lady she knew, Mrs. Whateverski. And now she was walking around checking up on everyone else.

Haze tapped down on the top of the bottle of anti-bacterial cream he'd smeared on the gauze swaddling Flaco's right thigh and set it back in its place inside the first aid kit. He looked up and saw the two old guys in their running gear at the bar now, swapping laughs and downing drinks. He shrugged. It was a storm party now, like the ones he'd seen in Canton when the last hurricane had blown B'more a kiss and moved on to Swamp Jersey and New York. Everybody was laughing and drinking and flipping the storm the bird. And here they were again, just laughing it off like they hadn't just seen two cops ripped apart by something impossible and run through a knee-deep flood as the city sank into the harbor.

He would have blamed it on silly white folks, but there was D, too, acting a fool.

Then he looked down at the Mossberg and decided it was time to reload it...if they had any more shells. It was only a matter of time before some other shit happened, right? They couldn't stay here for too long. Sooner or later, they'd have to get moving; there was no telling if or when the helicopter was coming back, and the third floor of any building after several earthquakes and aftershocks couldn't be considered safe ground, could it?

As if in answer to his question, the earth rumbled its response. The shotgun jumped off the table, then the table flipped. Someone screamed behind him. And suddenly the entire building lurched to the right.

Haze spun, already knowing the voice, already aware as he was that Jessie had been only a few feet away. He'd been listening to her conversation with the old lady, smiling despite himself as she'd rambled through her history. As he came around, he took it all in in a blink - the walls peeling away, the glass crashing down, the floors collapsing. The couple in the far corner disappeared in a flash of dust and thunder. Mrs. Whateverslowski went over without a sound, her fingers extended in a last desperate attempt to snag her phone. Then Haze dove right at the closest section of the building that was tearing itself apart and snagged the only thing he could: the sleeve of Jessie's hoodie.

And he slid right after her into the air.

Reflexes Haze thought he'd lost kicked in - feeling the pressure of the blindside blitz, ducking and twisting through outstretched hands and powering through arm tackles, reading the moves of everyone around him, and that touch - putting the ball right on target, on the fly, under pressure. He felt them blazing through his body again like a forgotten fire and he swung free, fingers locked on the nearest upright beam, feet dangling, and below him, Jessie wrapped in her hoodie, caught in it like a rat in the trap, the only thing keeping her from plunging two floors into the swirling ink of the expanded harbor formerly known as Thames Street.

"Haze!" she screamed, caught in the cottony clutches of the heather gray sweatshirt. The earth shook again, and Haze squeezed his fingers tight, refusing to let go.

"Jessie, hold on. Hold on." It's all he could get out; he was already breathless just from the - whatever the fuck that had just happened. His arms were on fire, and he felt like he was being ripped apart. If she could only climb up somehow, he thought. If he could only pull her in, flex with some superhuman strength that he knew he didn't possess and drag her up to what might one day be Woody's third story Caribbean bar again.

But that was not going to happen, he knew. His grip was already beginning to fizzle, and one of two things was going to happen: he was going to drop her and save himself, or they were both going to fall into whatever was waiting below. And that was going to happen soon. It was what it was, he thought. And maybe there was gonna be no culinary art school after all. Damien would take the seed money and go, and that would be the end of it.

And where was that fucker anyway? Long gone, money in hand, chasing dreams and pussy and leaving his friend...

"Hey!"

He felt hands on him, and when he looked up, he saw an unfamiliar face. Two actually, but one pair of hands were locked around his wrist, so he wasn't going to ask for introductions yet. "Let go. I gotcha," said the guy. Behind him and the other dude, Flaco was looking on, his one good hand hooked around the guy's belt, trying to keep him from going over the edge, too. He flashed a weak smile, his face pale underneath the bandages. Then Haze glanced down at Jessie again. He could see her still caught up in her own clothing, maybe the only thing that was keeping her from the stinking gray water below.

"Let go up here, Haze. We got you, amigo."

That wasn't Damien, he knew; that nigga didn't come back for nobody.

When he looked up again, Damien was still not there, no sweat pouring from his face, no hands on his wrist, no eyes locking on his friend's. He nodded and let go.

The guy above was true to his word, and they had him, a solid grip, pulling now, Flaco trying to give some kind of help from his angle. Haze groaned, his shoulders screaming. Then more hands came into play, grabbing him at the elbow. The earth trembled, threatening to shake them all loose, but they held on, and suddenly the hands moved to Haze's shoulder and his chest, pulling on whatever they could grab.

Haze grunted as he felt the searing pain in his right shoulder, the sudden shift of his grip, and then it was over. The pain was gone and the pressure in his shoulder with it. He took a deep breath, dropping to the floor as a shock of electricity jolted through his arms, tingling in his fingertips.

"Jessie," he whispered.

"We got her, man. Let go, Haze. We gotcha, amigo. It's all good." Flaco's voice was in his head, but Haze couldn't see anything but the floor as he lay face down on the splintered wood, gasping for breath and feeling the fire of his arms coming back to life. They'd been burning, going numb - it was hard to describe; all he knew was they were both about to rip off as they pulled him up, but for the moment, he was still whole.

"You done good." Flaco kneeled inches from his face. "You okay?"

Haze grunted and shifted, rolling over and sitting up with a little help from the cop. He waved off the proffered hand, his fingers still aching and stiff, then climbed to his feet when he was ready, flexing his shoulders and looking around. Faces laced with concern stared back - Flaco and the other guys he'd seen Jessie talking to - he hadn't gotten their names, but they seemed alright, about his dad's age and outfitted in running gear.

And then there was Jessie - she pulled herself up, breathless, her eyes full of tears. She swallowed and yanked the hoodie over her head, dropped it at her feet. Underneath it was a light blue tee with the letters PBR across the front. "Always hated that thing," she said and kicked it over the edge into the water.

"It didn't hate you," said Flaco, watching it drop over the edge.

"It served its purpose, I guess," said Haze, his eyes locked on hers now, relief washing through his system like a sudden high. "You okay?"

She nodded, clearly lying, and wiped away the tears, but he understood. He would've lied, too, he knew. His heart was still pounding in his chest, and the ache in both shoulders was dull but a reminder that they'd almost gone the way of the little old lady and the couple. The water might not be that deep, but who knew what else was down there? So, was he okay? Sure. Sure he was. They all were. As okay as anyone could be in this fucked up situation. Whatever had saved them - a raggedy old sweatshirt and an unlikely friend - well, he would take that.

"Then let's get the fuck outta here," said Flaco and he pushed the shotgun into Haze's hand. "You ready?"

Haze stared back at him, read the looks of the small group that stood there - Flaco, Jessie, the two guys who'd helped him up, and a handful of others huddled by the bar. They all seemed unprepared to do anything without his lead, except for performing a rescue, and that, he thought, would have to do.

"I guess so. Jessie?"

She nodded.

"And you guys?" He turned to the runners.

"Mike and Marty," said one. "And yeah, let's get out of here before the rest of this place comes down."

"Bet." Haze nodded. "I don't wanna do that shit again, hear?"

Everyone nodded and moved.

"Stay away from windows." He threw Jessie a smirk as he leaned down and gathered the bag of seed money. Shit was gonna work out; maybe. He shrugged it on as he waited for everyone to wind around the bar to the narrow staircase to the roof. Without even considering where they would go, the decision to leave Marley's behind was made. And maybe there was a rescue on the way.

"Promise." Jessie stopped at the foot of the stairs, pulling her backpack snug around her slender form. She waited while the others tromped up the steps, then turned and stared at him as he approached, but didn't move aside as he stopped next to her. Close, so close his fingers brushed hers, lingered against her skin, a new sort of fire coursing through his arm now.

"We're gonna be okay."

"Yeah." She stared up at him, then leaned up and pressed her lips to his.

Haze let her lean in, inhaling the kiss. She tasted of tequila and sweat and salt air. Her eyes, closed now, were rimmed in smeared make-up; her hair a rat's nest that no self-respecting Baltimore rat would own up to. But he smiled into the kiss, and tried not to think of how shitty he looked right then, too. How bad he smelled. What a pair! Like two corpses kissing at a funeral. A pretty girl kissing him while the city was drowning and twenty-five large in the bag. Whodda thunk it?

He couldn't stifle the laugh, and when she drew back, eyes open and searching, she echoed his laughter, a girly giggle. He drew back, a little embarrassed and a little pleased. It hadn't been as awkward as he thought it'd be.

"Not cool." The voice from the top of the stairs made Haze look up, his lips flattening out as the smile fell from his eyes. It was a voice he recognized but couldn't quite place until the face that went along with it came into view.

Rick oozed down the steps, his accusing gaze darting between the two.

"Not now, Rick." Jessie frowned at him.

"Oh, now is good. Now is when I find my girl sucking face with this dude. Who the fuck is he anyway?"

"His name is Haze," said Jessie, stepping in between them. "And he just saved, um, me."

Haze just looked on, letting Jessie take the lead. This was no time for some shit to come up. He eyed Rick up and down - no telling if he was armed, and that was the last thing they needed to deal with. Haze still had the shotgun in his right hand, but he kept it low, muzzle pointed at the ground. Whatever was about to happen, it was not getting fixed that way.

"What kinda name is that?"

"What do you care? Suddenly you noticed that I'm not standing next to you? You have your hand so far up Roxie's shorts it looks like you're giving her a colonoscopy."

"What's that supposed to mean?" Rick had reached the bottom of the stairs now, and he circled to his left, keeping his distance from Haze, but keeping Jessie in front of him.

"Google it."

"Hey now," he said, raising his arms in a shrug, "that was an us thing, a you and me thing. With Roxie. It was something we did together, remember? It was cool and fun, right baby?"

"Yeah, cool and fun. It was - that one time, and then you and her a few more times, I think. And you must have missed me not having it. For me, no, that much fun."

"Who's up for fun! Aw yeah, girl!" Suddenly Damien appeared at the top of the steps, waving a bottle of rum.

Damien whooped and bounded down the steps, but no one else was paying attention. Haze's eyes were on the closing space between Rick and Jessie. Rick stepped up, glaring but seemingly calm. Jessie didn't back down. She stared right back at him, all five foot nothing of her, looking up at his six-foot frame and his Medusa nest of black hair. The urge to say something, to step in somehow, was tugging hard at him, but Haze knew he couldn't. This wasn't his shit to get into, and Jessie was holding her own. In fact, as he stood there waiting to see what would happen, she leaned into Rick and then slowly, one hand raised, pushed him away.

"Not a chance, Rick. I don't know if you want to hit me or kiss me, but neither of those is an option. The only option you got is to get up those stairs and keep an eye on your prized heifer; with no bra, those udders are bound to attract a milkman or farmer soon. Hell, look at Damien."

Damien took a long swig of the rum and grinned like a fool. "I'm hoping that shit's chocolate milk. I love me some chocolate milk, girl." And with a guffaw, he disappeared back up the steps.

Rick watched him go, a blank expression on his face, then he gave Jessie and Haze a once-over before following Damien. "We'll talk later," he mumbled, as he thundered up the old wooden risers.

"Uh-huh." Jessie didn't turn to watch him go. She just stared straight ahead until Haze moved up beside her, the tips of his fingers brushing against the back of her hand. "She's been texting him for a while now, and he thinks I don't know about it."

Haze stared down at her, unsure of what to say or do. He'd kinda understood the situation from the start. She'd made it clear there was someone else, but suddenly things had changed. And then they'd changed again. And didn't he just need to take his money and run? Nothing was going the way they'd planned, and now this - this girl, and every time his fingertips brushed her skin...

"It's nothing to worry about, Haze," she said, turning and looking up at him. "He's nothing to worry about." Her hand twisted as she came around, and suddenly her fingers were lingering on his. "Cool?"

He nodded. "Bet." Pretty, he thought looking down at her, but...

Then just as Jessie climbed the first step, she spun and planted a kiss on him before he could even react, although his lips certainly knew what to do without being told. When she pulled away, her eyes twinkled like stars in the low light, and Haze felt a sudden urge to reach up and grab her, pull her close, and try it again on his own terms. But she was too quick, already dancing away, her voice echoing in the shadows.

"That was for saving my life. Now let's get going. We're missing the rescue party."

10

JESSIE CLIMBED THE stairs with a grin on her face, each step a little lighter as she neared the top. The fact that someone had risked his life to save her - well, for the first time since the day had begun, she felt like she was someone again.

Rick certainly hadn't contributed to that at all. How typical of him to suddenly appear and try to mark his territory. When was he gonna whip out his dick and piss on her leg? He'd done it often enough - not actually piss on her but see a guy flirting and step in to make his claim known. Meanwhile, at the other end of the bar, he "flirted for tips". What was good for the gander was decidedly not good for the goose. And he could go fuck himself.

Jesse's smile fell totally flat when she got a load of Fells Point from up on high, a real good look from one end to the other, and all that relationship bullshit went out the virtual window. She reached up and wiped the raindrops from her face and took a deep breath. Her little world, whatever it had been, was gone.

Before, when the helicopter was the only focus, Jessie had seen almost nothing of what was around them. Everything was right in front of her or non-existent, and that's what was necessary. She'd seen what she needed to see - Misha's dead body, the crabs bearing down on Mrs. Swaslowski, the way up to Woody's and a possible rescue, and Haze's face as he hung over the edge of the building and looked down at her. Now, she wished she could unsee what was right before her eyes as they inched across the rooftop, following the rest of their crew.

Fires burned to her left, all along the waterfront - probably another gas pipe ruptured. Heavy black smoke mixed with the morning fog and rain, mirroring the water that seethed in every direction, splashing monochromatic waves up over Thames Street and filling the air with the stink of charred wood and briny water. In front of them, the old City Pier, once famous for its role in Homicide: Life on the Streets, and then transformed into a swanky hotel, was nothing more than debris now, a massive pile of overpriced flotsam and concrete jetsam being swallowed by the oncoming waves. To the right, the entire square was underwater, random trees jutting up through the murk at odd angles like some eccentric art project. And behind them, away from the water, rooftop after rooftop sported people of all shapes and sizes - dozens all searching the skies and pointing at the two helicopters circling.

They kept moving, trying to get farther away from the water and toward a small group of people on the far side of the block. They climbed from building to building, the rowhomes all smashed together but some of the roofs partially collapsed, forcing them to zig left or zag right. Jessie watched the progress from the rear, keeping an eye on everyone, especially Haze, who walked within arm's reach, as if he was waiting for something else to happen. What would have been a one-minute walk on the sidewalk turned into a long, winding trip from one end of the block to the other, waiting for the next danger to present itself. Wood and shingles underfoot groaned with their weight, and each step became a test of faith. Would the roof collapse underneath them? What would happen if there was another tremor? Already the fire from the other end of the block down Thames was spitting flames into the air, belching even more smoke that swept low over the roofline with the changing wind. How quickly would it spread across to where they were?

Jessie wiped her face again, tasting the sweat as well as the rain, then whipped her backpack around and fished out her lucky O's cap and pulled it on. The orange was still bright, but the black Oriole silhouette was fading - too many games sitting in the bleachers under the hot summer sun, but what she wouldn't do for that sun now, she thought.

Blinking away the last of the raindrops, she eyed the other members of their ragtag group and the others that waited at what seemed to be their destination, the northernmost rooftop before the chasm that would be Lancaster again. There were eleven of them marching across the rooftops - four women and seven men, and about a dozen or so ahead, all focused on the two circling helicopters and screaming and hollering and jumping up and down. One of the choppers, a red and blue number, descended and hovered over a building a few blocks up. They watched as it dropped a ladder down and the three people on the rooftop scrambled up. Voices all around battered her ears with growls and groans as they finally reached the end of the line.

"They're being rescued?! Why didn't they come get us?"

"I'm tweeting about this as soon as the internet is back, and I'm tagging the mayor."

"I'm moving to the fucking county; shit like this doesn't happen in the county."

Jessie sighed and slowed up just out of reach of the angry mob, her own eyes locked on the helo as it rose into the air and slid north. She shrugged and plopped down on one of the silver AC units and tuned in to the chatter that sprang up when the two groups merged.

What was everyone doing when the quake hit? Whose cat ran off across the roof and would Mr. Fluffy be seen again? Was he chipped? Why hadn't the city warned them about the earthquakes? Didn't they have an emergency action plan? Had anyone seen another Get Pink flip flop? The left one? Why were they getting such shitty cell service from the roof? Did anyone think there'd be earthquake specials at the local bars later? Where did that guy get rum and was there any more beer in the silver cooler those other guys brought up?

Haze paused just shy of them, too, dropping down next to Jessie, his eyes searching. "What now? Wait for a ride?"

"Dunno." She wanted to shrug again, but she didn't have the energy.

They were just winging this whole thing, weren't they? She nodded at Flaco, happy not to be the authority figure in the group, although the cop, battered and bandaged as he was, didn't look like much of an authority figure. His hat was gone, as was his radio, and his blue-black shirt was ripped open in several places, revealing blood-stained gauze. His hands rested on his knees as he eased himself down onto the slick roofing tiles. Before he was even settled, he was surrounded, and the questions flowed over him like the water below would, words dripping with anger and fear threatening to drown him until he stood up again, a grimace on his face, and pushed through the little crowd and past Haze without a word.

Jessie glared at the little group, then turned to Flaco, wrapping her arm around his shoulders, feeling his body tremble with each step. His face was pale and dripping with sweat, and his chest heaved. She pulled him along a little farther as the complainers turned, looking for answers. Flaco needed to sit down, and he needed water. He wasn't going to be able to help or stand up to the little mob that was forming if he kept going like this. Already his skin felt clammy and hot. He was going to need some serious medical attention soon, more than the patch job they'd done.

Jessie looked back as she eased Flaco down onto the silver metal of the rooftop cooling unit; Haze lifted his hand to stop the angry group, stepping between them and Flaco and Jessie. "Hold up, yo."

"What's the cop doing up here? Shouldn't he be helping with a rescue or something?"

"Where's his radio?"

"What's with that shotgun? You a cop?"

Jessie rummaged through her pack - there were the two bottles of water, and Flaco needed them more than she ever did. Her back to the crowd, eyes on the teetering cop, she unscrewed the top of the bottle and listened to Haze's voice. He was calm, used uncomplicated words, even if he let slip some profanity. "The officer is hurt. He can't fix any of this shit by himself. He's just one guy. You gotta step up now."

"Hey, I pay taxes, pal," blurted one of the guys - it sounded like that six-foot tall, muscled guy in the black tank top and backwards trucker hat that had wandered over. He looked like a douche, and he sounded like one, too, more muscles than brains. "I know my rights."

Jessie glanced back and saw the big guy step up like he was gonna do something. He stopped a few feet from Haze and gave it his best Friday morning beer-goggles glare, the can of Natty Boh half crushed in his jerk-it hand.

"Right to what? Not be dead? Not get snapped in half by a giant crab like his partners? They're all dead." Haze hadn't made a move, kept his voice steady. He just stared back, stance set but easy. One hand was half in his pocket; the other hand held the shotgun, and he kept it hanging loose, aimed at the ground.

Douche guy kept going, cranking up his volume. "You high, bro? Smoke a bowl before you came out today?"

"Ain't nobody got time for that, yo." Suddenly Damien appeared, pushed through the crowd, and stood by his boy, one hand gripping his shoulder. "We don't need none of that Yuppie white boy 'I ain't had my latte yet' bullshit. Shit's real. Mothafuckas is dead back there, dog, and three of them is cops. They saved us; we saved this one. Now we gotta save our own asses. Either get with the program or get your ass dead."

"Dead from what?" said the douche, taking one more step forward, but he stopped there when he saw the shotgun in Haze's hand twitch.

"From that," said Haze as he pointed, his left hand up and aiming over the near edge of the roof at the flooded sea that had been Broadway Square. Heads turned. Eyes followed. In the middle of what would be the weekly farmer's market the next day, a few massive shapes sloshed about in the floodwaters, bluish shells bobbing like corks while massive claws snapped at empty air.

"Crabs, bro," said Damien. "Big fucking Baltimore crabs. Blue softshells back with a vengeance. Ain't you been paying attention or them six packs of Boh been on your mind."

Muscles stared down at the impossible made possible like a human statue, mouth gaping like he's just seen a skinny chick squat 350 on the rack, while a few others stood behind him and passed around fresh cans of Boh.

"Ain't nothing but a thing," one of them said.

"We got enough beer to go round til the rescue, bro; no worries," said another, and he spun around and sat down on the dented, silver cooler at his feet.

Muscles stared and took a last sip, held out his hand for another. "Beer me," he said, and his wish was fulfilled.

Jessie shrugged and handed Flaco the second bottle of water. Not a threat, not when the booze was flowing. It was the Fells Point way. If you can't do it with beer, it ain't worth doing. And suddenly the moment was over; beer and something amazing had won over their short attention spans.

That and the sudden solidarity of the two men who'd appeared out of nowhere had gotten them this far. Where they'd come from and who they were was still mostly a mystery, but she'd seen some things that had more than impressed her.

Jessie looked at Damien, who stood nearby with his hands in the pockets of the overalls he was still sporting, the black bag over his right shoulder. The bottle of rum was gone, but he seemed steady, and he'd stepped up to support his friend, so she wasn't going to complain. Haze waited next to him, not a muscle out of place, not a twitch to make anyone nervous about that shotgun - cool as a cucumber colada on a hot summer day, and this one was a scorcher, so to speak. His matching bag was slung across his back now, covering up the number seven and dispelling the defined "V" shape that ran from his shoulders to his waist.

The rising chopper whoop-whooped right over their heads, causing a couple of them to duck, dispelling the moment. Jessie blinked and Haze was spinning around, the seat of his pants disappearing from view. She frowned and turned back to Flaco, who was still sipping steadily, and listened to the blades whooshing through the air, wondering how long they'd be on the roof. Was that the only way out of this nightmare? A chopper rescue? If only he'd brought a radio of some sort. And would it matter? There were dozens upon dozens of people on the roofs all around them, and no way to know how many of them were seriously hurt or dying.

She watched the rescue swing around over the harbor and disappear into the low clouds overhead. Then suddenly the second chopper swung in over the rooftops, its thundering blades nearly drowning out the screams and pleads of the people around her. It hovered and descended, this time so close they could feel the rush of wind off the blades, but so far away when it landed across the gaping chasm of churning water a block north.

Jessie shook her head. It just wasn't their day, she thought. But before she could even open her mouth to voice it, her radar was already dropping the helicopter rescue and picking up something much more important: a whiff of smoke. And where there was smoke, ...

"Haze." Her voice was flat, a calm that even surprised her. When he turned around, she nodded back the way they'd come. "We can't stay here anymore."

"Fuck me."

She heard the snap, crackle and pop of flame devouring wood for the first time then, and when the wind shifted again, she smelled the bubbling tar. It was mesmerizing, like a great beast closing in, devouring everything in its path. Gnarled fingers of black smoke gushed from new orifices as shingles and crossbeams were consumed, and suddenly the air was filled with another roar as the building next to Woody's caved in on itself, spewing bright tongues of liquid flame into the air.

One look between them said it all.

"Go!" Jessie was up as the words burst out of her mouth, her hands reaching for the resting policeman. She pulled on his sleeve, yanking him out of his daze. "Come on, Flaco."

"Move your ass, dude," said Haze, leaning in to help get the cop up.

Jessie looked back just then, and her heart tumbled into her stomach. Woody's was already gone and the next nearest house was already being consumed. They all knew the routine in these ancient but updated rowhomes constructed in the late 1700s under the watchful eye of Lord Fells' shipbuilding empire. Everyone here lived in an historic fiery death trap complete with tax breaks and a small chance of going out via impromptu cremation. The only real solution was multiple fire alarms...or sitting on the rooftops watching the block consumed by flames. They had plenty of warning now as the fire raced toward them. The only issue was where they would go next.

"Move, you assholes. We're getting off this roof now," she bellowed, but no one seemed to notice. She dragged Flaco forward, Haze right in step with her, voices rising behind them from the people focused on the rescue a block away. She ignored them, ignored Flaco's groaning limp and the mumbled words in Spanish that had to be profanity or bitching about the pain, she decided. Haze was silent, but Damien's voice trailed behind them, as well, fuming but coming along, grumbling about the lack of rum and rescue choppers.

Underneath her aching feet Jessie felt the roof tremble, or was it just her legs giving out? She couldn't decide and didn't have time to care as she climbed over yet another short wall and pulled the policeman after her. Another choking plume of smoke swept over them, blinding her and doubling her over in a fit of coughing. She stumbled on, one arm clutching Flaco, the other flailing at the suffocating smog, hoping they weren't too close to the roof edge. A few tentative steps and then it was gone again, the damp wind sweeping the smoke away like it was nothing more than a warning.

A few paces away Rick and Roxie stood together, watching them come. Rick opened his mouth to speak, but Jessie shut him down with a look and a few choice words: "Don't wanna hear it. Come with us, or else." He didn't reply, and Roxie only emitted a protest peep when Jessie shoved by her. "Deal with it, bitch," she grumbled, and then all she could hear were footsteps behind them until they reached the edge of the final house and looked down onto a rooftop at least a dozen feet or so below.

"Now what?" Haze moved in beside Jessie and leaned up under Flaco's shoulder, taking some more of his weight and giving her a little break.

In front of them was the sloping roof of Jimmy's, an old diner of sorts that was, in Jessie's opinion, the best place to snag a real American breakfast. Too many other spots sported over-fancied menus, but Jimmy's kept it easy and kept it right for the queasy tummy and the empty wallet. The pancakes were her thing, and the rest of their breakfast was right on target, too - even the scrapple. She stared down at the black shingles and thought about the earthquake and how it'd ruined a perfect pancake Friday.

"Extra syrup?" she muttered.

"Huh?"

"Nothing. We gotta get down from here; down to Jimmy's and then down on the street."

"Then what? And what about them?" Haze nodded at the bluish shells bobbing in the square, as if they were waiting for someone foolish enough to dip a toe. "Looks like the water's getting deeper, too."

Jessie shrugged. "All I know is if we stay here, we're going to be Jimmy's special barbecue tomorrow."

"We gotta get to Patterson Park," said Rick as he sidled up next to Jessie, keeping his distance from Haze. "High ground and open ground - we get out of the water and away from buildings, right?" He scanned their faces for approval, but Jessie kept her gaze fixed ahead. "That river down there is Lancaster Street. We need to go East," he said, pointing away from the square, "and then cut up to the north, where we can move up to high ground."

Haze nodded. "Yeah, that's good, but how far is it?"

"It's gonna be a hike in this shit, but maybe ten minutes under normal conditions."

Jessie glanced sideways at Rick, eyes narrow and hard for a moment. "It's a good idea, but no more bullshit from you. Not a fucking peep. You're in or you're out. Pick one."

Rick stared out across the square for a moment.

"Fire!" came a voice from behind them before he could even reply, and suddenly the rooftop shook from rapidly approaching footsteps and one dragged cooler.

Jessie turned and all she could see was a black wall of smoke racing toward them, consuming the fleeing fugitives and turning their world suddenly back to night. The roof shuddered and groaned like a great beast just as the gates of Hell opened up underneath them and the air was filled with screams.

11

"HAZE." JESSIE'S VOICE seemed far away, hollow as if she was in a tunnel. "Haze."

He took a deep breath, trying to clear away the cobwebs, but it was as if the fog had slithered into his head and wrapped itself around his brain. He floated in it, on it, like a giant mattress lulling him back to sleep. If she would only shut up for a second, he could roll over and drift off again.

"Haze!"

Haze blinked, saw stars shooting by, bright lights that hurt his eyes. He blinked again and colors swirled in his vision, then they solidified into the flat silver of an air conditioning duct and Flaco's black hair. He took a deep breath and pushed, shifting the policeman's body to the side. He sat up slowly, fighting back against the dull fog that threatened to envelop him again. His stomach churned, empty or not, but he kept moving until he was around on his knees, bent over and battling the heaves.

Deep breaths through his nose, trying to see through to the other side, trying to breathe through the nausea, then he felt a cool hand on the back of his neck, saw a familiar pair of boots appear next to him. A voice in his ear.

"You okay?" Jessie knelt, her hand still against his skin, reassuring.

"Yeah, yeah." He hesitated, taking a deep breath in through his nose, focusing on the cool fingers. "The roof. Flaco. He's okay?"

Jessie shifted. The hand lifted away from Haze's neck. He missed it immediately. He watched her out of the corner of his eye, determined not to turn his head at all. Every little movement had him questioning the capacity of his stomach. She knelt over the cop, turning his head to the side and pressing her fingers against his throat, holding her palm under his nose. A moment later, she pulled her hand away and plopped down next to Haze, leaning into him a little.

"No. Not okay."

"What?"

"He's dead." Her voice trembled when she said it. "Broken neck, I think."

Then Haze vomited. Whatever was still in his stomach spewed from his mouth and splattered across the asphalt roof between his hands. He coughed and heaved again, mostly spit and what was left of the tequila. "Fuck," was the only word that came out between breaths and the contractions in his stomach; he swallowed whatever words might come after that. They wouldn't matter now, not to Flaco, wherever he was. He'd done what he could to protect them, and they him. First cop he'd ever had a conversation with that didn't involve threats of jail time, someone getting frisked and asked if they had drugs.

Flaco had given him a gun and leaned on him. Needed his help.

The rest, they'd always looked at him like he was already guilty, like he was just standing on the corner waiting to commit some kind of crime if only the cops would fuck off. Even in Canton, surrounded by white folks with their money and cars, girls in short dresses and guys in cargo shorts - wasn't that a crime of some kind? But the cops always eyed him. Other than his Air Force One's, he'd left his Westside self on the Westside. He'd hiked up his pants and dropped the swagger in his walk, the one that he'd needed to cruise the streets west of MLK with confidence. But still the cops looked at him when he stepped out to his old green Civic at oh dark thirty in the morning with a lil paper in his pocket; they left him with only one idea in his head: stay away from the cops.

Armed robbery and now this... "I killed him." Haze looked up at Jessie through crystalline tears. Behind her, smoke blotted out the sky, and the building they'd been on belched flames from every orifice.

"Not your fault," she said.

"He's dead."

"Not because of you. Who put those bandages on him?

Haze wiped his mouth, took a deep breath, catching a whiff of the burning air. "The fire?"

Jessie looked up, eyes scanning past his face. "It's still eating that house, but if it jumps..."

"What about him?"

"Leave him. If the fire jumps that brick wall, ... Gotta leave him."

"We can't," he said, pushing himself up, grimacing as he took a little weight on his left leg.

"Yes, we can. We can't carry him. Jesus, can you even walk?"

Haze stared at the solemn face of the fallen policeman. "Yeah," he said. "I been hurt worse."

"Then let's get these people moving," said Jessie, and she spun around.

The mob, battered cooler and all, was scattered on the roof of Jimmy's like a game of fifty-two card pick-up. Haze looked around as they slowly began to come around, some of them already up and jabbering. He tuned it out and just watched Jessie as she went around to check on the human flotsam, getting them up. The runners looked okay, checking each other over. The girl in the bright pink robe and now just one matching slipper pointed and said something to the guy still clinging to his cooler. He shook his head and shrugged. Muscles stood behind them, his face and shirt smeared with soot as he chatted with a few other guys no worse for the wear. It didn't look like anyone was really hurt, and Flaco was the only casualty. Their group was intact, but Haze wasn't sure if they were ready for the next step. Hell, he shrugged, he wasn't sure if he was either.

Haze took stock of the rest of their own crew from One-Eyed Mike's, all of them up now and moving. Damien held his phone in one hand, off in his own world at the edge of the low roof, snapping pictures of the square. Rick and Roxie huddled a few feet away, Rick whispering something in her ear while she looked anxiously from the water below to what was left of the three-story rowhome behind them. Then Jessie was back from her rounds, waiting a few feet away, her eyes fixed on the rowhome, too, her fingers caressing a slim silver automatic like it was a good friend.

"Yours?" Haze indicated the gun with a nod.

"Yeah. Figured it might come in handy in a pinch."

"Those things have quite a pinch." He nodded past her to the water.

"So does Eleanor here." She winked and holstered the pistol under her left shoulder. "Let's get off this roof."

"Bet," he said, his eyes drifting back down to Flaco's unmoving body. His silver badge gleamed wet in the rainy morning, and on a whim, Haze reached down and snatched it from his chest. He stared at the badge for a moment, tracing the engravings with his thumb, reading the words written in black letters across the front: To Serve and Protect. Then pocketed it and looked around for the shotgun and his black bag. It was as much as he could carry for now. "Sorry, cabrón," he whispered and then stood up and found Jessie moving everyone to the edge of the roof again.

Haze checked over the shotgun. They'd had a few shells left, and he'd pushed them all into the receiver back in Woody's. It would have to do. Hopefully it would get them to the park. If they moved quietly. If those giant fuckers weren't crabbing around down there waiting for them in the street. He could only see the big ones from Jimmy's roof; the gray-black water covered everything else. Were there others? The smaller ones they couldn't see? Ones they wouldn't even know were there until they hit the water and felt the little pinchers tearing at them?

He'd figure it out, he thought, moving out, because Jessie was already getting some of them down off the roof.

The climb down would have been easy, Haze decided, if his leg didn't hurt like a bitch. But he'd played hurt before, and this game wasn't over. Two half-submerged dumpsters squatted underneath the edge of the roof about six feet down, offering them a way down to the street. The water was about waist high now, he figured. It was going to be a slog to the end of the street, and slower if they managed to alert those things in the square. Slower still if his knee was as bad as it felt. But what choice was there?

"You ready?" He felt Jessie's presence. Then Damien leaned over the edge next to him.

"That shit stanks." He pulled back and turned to his friend. "You know black folks don't swim."

"Better doggie paddle your ass down that Yellow Brick Road then, dog, 'cause we off to see the wizard."

"Yeah, crabs and quakes and Hepatitis, oh my!"

"Bet." Haze stared at Jessie, cracked a smile. "Now, let's get this group of misfits to the Emerald City."

"Grab your boy," said Damien, his eye on Jessie. "And that honey."

"My boy? He'll be fucking you before he fucks me again." Jessie turned around with a frown, headed over to Rick and the rest of the spectators.

"Oh shit, Haze. You gotta live lil white girl there."

"Ain't mine yet, dog. Got some cards to play yet."

"Oh, I don't know 'bout that. You did save her cute little ass back there. Look at it." He sighed, shook his head. "That shit tight."

"Yeah, yeah. Shut your pie hole, dog. You're slobbering on your shirt there." Haze turned back, watching where Damien's eyes were locked, smiled to himself, then took in the whole scene. Muscles was handing over his shirt to Pink Robe Princess; it seemed that was the only thing she had on besides a pair of lime green cheekies, and with

Jessie pointing down toward the water as she spoke, maybe she decided that less was more. Better alive in a cheap, dirty t-shirt than pinched in half in an expensive Victoria's Secret robe, which she dropped at her feet. Gave Muscles a chance to flex anyway.

The guy with the cooler looked none too happy, but that was probably because he was out of beer. He handed out three and popped the tab on the last one, throwing it back like a hero, and flicked the empty out into the churning chaos below. The runners were already climbing down. Rick was in Roxie's ear, tugging her hand and inching her towards the edge. The rest of them were shuffling over now, maneuvering around until they were all lined up like paratroopers about to make a grave jump.

Jessie was the last one back. "Ok, we're ready. I told them where we were going, what was waiting for us...and to keep their mouths shut unless they wanted to be their own special kind of crab cake."

Haze smiled back at her, felt the first pang of hunger. "Don't remind me that I haven't eaten yet today."

"Maybe if you play your cards right, I'll let you buy me lunch."

"Bet." Haze winked, then turned his attention to the small crowd that had gathered, counting heads - lucky number nineteen. "Okay, keep moving, people. Everybody down in the water," he said, pointing down Lancaster away from the square and the threat bobbing there. "Then we're working our way up to high ground at Patterson Park. We move quickly and quietly and watch out for more of those bastards over there." He nodded back towards the square. The number of bobbing monsters seemed to have grown while they waited. There were clearly a few handfuls now. "We good?"

"No, we not good," came a voice with a mocking tone. "We not good at all, man. Who the fuck are you anyway? And don't tell me you're the cops or flash that badge I saw you take off that one back there." It was Muscle's other friend, a skinny dude with a beard and black t-shirt that read "Bo Knows Boh". He stood in front of his shirtless friend and Cooler Guy like a Hipster disaster movie hero. The rest of the crew they'd found on the roof drinking and watching helicopters circle was standing behind them like a little gang of Happy Hour thugs, and none of them seemed pleased with what Haze had said.

He looked from face to face, reading the concern or scowls or whatever half-drunken stupor masked their faces.

"Me? I'm nobody. Just trying to help."

"That why you took that cop's badge? That why you have his shotgun? I see that's police issue."

Haze stared, swallowed.

"None of your shit, pencil neck," said Jessie, stepping up. "Let's just get the hell off this roof. Did you see the fire?" Jessie pointed, and every head turned to look back where they'd come from, and Haze could see the recognition in their faces. "You know how fast that shit can burn through these old rowhomes. And what if there's another quake? We need to get off the roof here, too. So, if you're done measuring dicks..."

Silence, both groups eyeing each other. Haze kept the shotgun barrel pointed down, tried to will himself to look non-threatening. He didn't have time for the bullshit, but could he leave them behind? His eye wandered back to the body clad in police blues just the other side of the silver ducting. Or was it really any of his business what happened to these people? He had the money and a gun, and he had a path out. If they wanted to stay and die... Fuck 'em, right?

"You don't have to follow me or listen to me at all," said Haze, the words pouring out before he even realized they were in his head - felt like another late game huddle pep talk. "But I'm getting out of here with my friends. Now we couldn't save Flaco, or the other cops, and we can't take them with us, but maybe we can do what he was trying to do - get us all to safety."

Before anyone could even answer, he turned and dropped down to the dumpster, grimacing when a sharp pain lanced up his leg, but he reached up for Jessie right away. She was close behind, the silver pistol tucked into her waistband as if she'd seen too many movies. Damien was next, and he turned to help ease down Roxie with a big grin on his face, his big paws all over her fat ass as she came down. Haze sighed and scrambled down into the water as quietly as he could, feeling relieved when the cool water swirled around his knee. He felt lighter suddenly, buoyant in ways that physics couldn't explain, and then he was helping Jessie down again, watching her shudder when the water lapped up against her legs.

"Cold?"

She shook her head. "Hospital as soon as we're outta here. Clean harbor 2024, my ass."

"Then let's get you outta his shit right away, sister," said Damien, climbing down beside her. He repeated the earlier procedure and helped Roxie down, Rick looking down from atop the nearest dumpster, and looking none too pleased with where Damien's hands were on the dismount. Roxie, on the other hand, purred.

Haze rolled his eyes and looked past the hands-on flirtation toward the square. He could see a couple of shapes moving, but none of them seemed to be coming this way. Maybe they could get away after all, and hopefully there would be nothing in their path. The crabs seemed to be coming from the construction site, and if there weren't any between them and the park, they'd be set.

"Now what?" said Jessie.

Haze turned to look at her, but movement in the corner of his eye spun him around, and he watched the battered cooler sail through the air like a silvery comet until it crashed with a hollow splat onto the churning waves a dozen yards away. A drunken woot echoed down from the roof overhead, and he looked up to find Cooler Guy and Hipster Disaster Movie Hero high fiving before climbing down to the dumpsters.

Just then a bluish-black shell bobbed to the surface of the gray waves a few yards away and swiveled around towards the group climbing down into the water. Haze watched as rivulets of brackish liquid trickled down the monster's shell and fell like rain. Then it lurched forward.

"Run!" said Haze, and he raised the shotgun.

<h1 style="text-align:center">12</h1>

"GO! GO! GO!" JESSIE croaked and started shoving people past her as she reached into her holster and pulled out the Sig Sauer, feeling the cool metal in her hot palm. She sloshed away from the little crowd, and raised the pistol as the monster came on, waves washing the dented cooler aside as more of their group climbed down off the roof, screaming and yelling as the blue-brown behemoth squeezed into the alley street between two SUVs.

"Get the fuck out of here," shouted Haze and suddenly Jessie felt his hand around her waist.

"Let go," she yelled and tried to aim at the advancing creatures, then suddenly she was jerked off her feet and propelled backwards.

"Fuck that," Haze growled. "We're moving now, and you're going, too. Not leaving you behind." He pulled her along a few more backward steps, and finally Jessie couldn't look any more as the crab broke through the narrow gap and closed on the three stragglers just down from the dumpster. One claw swept the top of the waves, crunching one of the guys she hadn't yet met against the rusted dumpster. His body disappeared under the waist-high waves, but the monster didn't even pause. The other claw caught another around the waist, and he broke in two like a crusty French bread, screaming for his savior until he, too, disappeared beneath the waves. The last of the three just froze in place, back to the oncoming disaster he didn't want to see coming.

Jessie gave up and turned around, not willing to see his end. She waded forward as quickly as she could, her hands propelling her forward like paddles.

There was a short splash, a hollow thud of claw on water, and the familiar warbling rolled out over the waves like a wolf's howl.

"They're gone." It was all she could think as she focused on the path before her and the terrified figures scrambling over rubble and through the black water.

"Keep going, Jessie. We're gonna be okay."

But the crab was gaining in the narrow lane - she could hear it closing. Maybe it had better hydrodynamics. Maybe the current was accelerating it along. Maybe eight giant legs were better than two, but either way, the brownish-blue thing kept coming, leaving a wake behind it like a speed boat. Only this vessel had two massive claws that reached out with each lurch forward. Jessie glanced back, saw them snap at the open air and come together with a nasty crack. This fast wading just wasn't going to work. What was behind them was faster and hungrier than even Haze.

"Head to the left," said Haze, taking her hand and pulling her toward a mountain of debris, where several of the rowhomes on Lancaster had collapsed and their facades had spilled into the street. There were even a few small trees down nearby, and maybe they could use it for cover. Maybe that would slow down the thing behind them a little. Damien was already climbing up as they half-swam/half-ran to the destroyed home. He turned around and raised his own pistol, tracking back past the two, and fired from above. Jessie ducked, half-stumbling forward as she heard the bullets whizzing overhead.

"What the fuck?!"

"Run! It's right behind you!" Damien didn't bother to look down or point; he just aimed and fired from his perch again and again until he'd finished the clip. Then he quickly loaded a second and fired again.

Jessie cursed under her breath the whole way, but behind them, she could hear the crab's eerie whine and the bullets hitting home. It was so close. She didn't have to look back; she could feel the waves as it crashed forward. And then she felt Haze's momentum catching her, his hands around her waist as he propelled her forward and up onto the closest concrete blocks. Damien tucked his pistol away and jumped down and Jessie caught his hand, pulling as he swung her up and onto the chunks of brick and concrete, then they spun back for Haze.

"Fuck," she said, letting out a shriek at what she saw, her hand flying to the holster again.

The crab towered over Haze, coming on like an aquatic Mike Tyson, its claws raised for a powerful one-two punch.

"Behind you!" screamed Jessie just as the first massive claw fell. Haze saw it just in time and dodged left, throwing himself into the deadly waves. The claw smashed into concrete and brick, sending up shards of both like shrapnel. The second claw came down and black water splashed everywhere as if a meteor had hit the ocean. But Haze was already up and scrambling away, coughing and sputtering, wading into the middle of the street away from the monster as Jessie began to fire. Damien's pistol sang in harmony with her silver Sig, and they pounded the creature. "The eyes," she shouted. "Go for the soft meat!"

The crab warbled again, in rage or agony - there was no way to tell as it turned toward its fleeing prey. Haze was still circling, barely keeping the shotgun above the water, his other hand steadying himself on the wall of fallen debris that grew higher before it finally subsided and a path around opened up. The crab kept pace, its shell scraping against the concrete as it swam around, claws poised for another swipe.

Gunshots echoed along the narrow corridor, then everything went silent.

"Out," said Damien.

"Me, too." Jessie stared at her Sig in disbelief. She hadn't ever really planned to have something to shoot at. She'd only brought the gun along because she liked to carry it; it made her feel safe. She never really thought ammo would be an issue in an earthquake. But what now? The crustacean had barely slowed, and they'd put at least two dozen rounds in it between them.

"Hurry, Haze. Hurry," she screamed as she picked her way over the fallen building, trying to keep her balance, looking for something to use as a weapon. But Haze had one of his own still and maybe a few shells left. Jessie saw the grimace on his face as he turned and raised the shotgun, and she froze in place, staring. But he didn't shoot. He waited, and she gritted her teeth as the monster shambled around the edge of the debris and found its prey. "Haze!" she cried, and he let go with a blast point blank. Then another and another, pumping the shotgun rounds into the mewling monstrosity until it staggered, and the Mossberg's trigger went "click."

"I'm out," he said and dropped the shotgun. It let out a sinister hiss when it hit the murky water, and then it was gone.

"Damn, dog. That was some tight monster movie shit. You could be an action hero." Damien beamed at his boy from the small mountain of debris next to Jessie. "Look out, Will Smith; here come Haze."

"Well, we don't have any more ammo, but I bet I could find some Old Bay and a few crab forks in this mess. You still hungry?" Jessie smiled and climbed down. "Maybe a couple bibs, too. Don't wanna mess up our outfits." She giggled as she eased herself into the water, shocked that she was cracking jokes. She could feel the tears behind her eyes just waiting for their moment.

She looked down at the black-gray water and took a deep breath, inhaling the stinking harbor. "Is this global warming? Are the sea levels rising? Or are we sinking?"

Haze shrugged.

"No time for exchanging recipes and fashion tips, folks," said Damien, still above them on top of his mountain. He pointed back the way they'd come, toward something that had narrowed his eyes. "More hungry mothafuckas coming this way. Crabs on the go, and we got no ammo. We gots to jet."

"How many?" Jesse shifted her stance, trying to peek around the edge of the debris, but she couldn't see much.

"All of them? I dunno. Three. Four. Make that four or...well, five now."

"Five or do you need a calculator?" Haze looked up at his friend. "Pull off your shoes and socks if it's a big number."

"Oh, suck deez two nuts, nigga. We gots a fucking legion of problems coming our way right now, and I can count to five without toes."

"Who cares how many there are," said Jesse, interrupting and waving for Damien to come down. "We have no ammo, and we just lost three guys back there."

"Three guys as was too damn slow."

Jesse hit Damien with an icy glare that shut his mouth. "It doesn't matter. We've got to go now, right?"

He nodded.

"Then let's go. Everyone else is already way ahead."

But when they turned, they found that wasn't true. The whole group had stopped and was watching in the waist deep water, even cheering. The only thing that was missing was the popcorn. Perhaps they'd watched the whole Battle of Lancaster Street, maybe to see a black man eaten by a crab, instead of the other way around. There was no telling, but they weren't halfway to Patterson Park and high ground; that much was obvious. They were standing in the middle of another debris field between three collapsed houses on the opposite side of the street - standing and staring like a bunch of spectators at an O's game.

"Move your asses," said Jesse, practically growling, and she pointed past them down Lancaster. "Fucking go! We gotta get to the park. You can watch the rest of this shit when they make a shitty TV movie out of it."

"Shit, who's gonna play me?" said Damien, dropping into the water and sloshing after her. "Denzel? Nah, too old now. Eddie Murphy, comic genius? But the crabs don't talk; he only does movies where animals talk. How 'bout Chris Rock? I mean, I'm fucking hilarious, right? Oh shit, no, Ice Cube, baby. Yeah, Ice Cube would play me."

"How about the guy who played Urkel in Family Matters?" said Jessie, winking at Haze.

He laughed out loud. "She pegged ya, D."

"How about you?" said Haze, eyeing Jessie.

Jessie glanced over as she reached the second fallen house and pulled herself up over the half wall of bricks and broken sheet rock. "Emma Watson, of course." She threw Haze a sly grin and topped the wall.

Haze nodded and climbed up after her. "Nice choice." Then the smile that had wrinkled his lips dropped away as that familiar sound warbled across the flooded streetscape. He turned and looked back, pulling Jessie's gaze around with him.

The crabs had rounded the first wall of debris. They pushed past their fallen kin without any sort of recognition and came on, claws waving, sloshing back and forth in a sort of wave-driven shuffle. They were quick and subtly so, whether it was the water masking their speed or the way they seemed to exert no effort. But before Jessie knew it, they were only a few yards away.

"Run!" It was a foolish thing to say, she knew, because they'd been fools to stand and watch the monsters come at them instead of staying ahead, but there was nothing for it now. Something about the whole situation continued to cry out that it was all just a dream, that she was trapped in a movie or a book, that at some point the narrator would stop and go to commercial break and get her out of there for a quick nap in her trailer. But that just wasn't happening. There really were giant, car-sized crabs coming down the street at them with claws as big as dining room tables. And if she didn't stay focused, she or her new friends might be on the menu.

They danced around the fallen walls, random pieces of furniture and appliances, and pushed through to the other side just at Ann

Street. The rest of their crew had already passed the corner and were nearing the park on Wolfe. Jessie yelled ahead for them to keep going, then risked a glance back. The crabs were making short work of the obstacle themselves, and they'd soon be through. What was keeping them alive, it seemed, was sheer luck and a little firepower, one of which was fresh out, and the other was nearing empty. How would they kill these next ones? Or would they even be able to get away without outside help? Those thoughts were turning over in her head as she slogged forward, slowing a little, feeling exhaustion creeping into her legs. Behind them the things were fast, strong, and their bodies worked with the environment. They fucking practically floated, like boats gliding across the surface of the water with their eight legs propelling them forward.

Suddenly she thought of crab legs and Old Bay and all the possibilities for the summer. Would she ever get down to Captain James and crack crabs on the dock again? Or were they going to crack her? What a revenge story! Epic fail...unless you were a crab.

At the end of the street, the water seemed deeper, but Jessie understood. They were closer to the water than they'd been with the way the harbor wrapped around Fells Point. At the corner of Wolfe and Lancaster, there was really only one option: go left. Right was a dead end back into Fells and eventually back to the block that was burning down behind them, or the water which stretched down the street. Straight led them to the marina and more water that was pouring in. So left it was.

Rick, it seemed, had already taken the group left, but they hadn't gotten far when Jessie, Haze and Damien rounded the corner. He looked back from his position in front of the post office and waved them on.

"What the hell, Rick?! We gotta keep moving. They're right behind us." Jessie pulled up short a few feet away, breaths coming in heavy gasps now. There was running and there was running in waist-deep water—they didn't do that latter kind of training in Body Pump.

"Can't," said Rick, and he turned his attention back to the huge shutter-like doors that marked the entrance to the post office. They had shifted with the quake and hung slightly apart. "Ashley cut her foot on something, and the beer cooler guy, Seth, can barely walk. He's fucking drunk." He pointed at the two offenders and scowled. "And Roxie's exhausted."

"So am I," said Haze, stepping up. "We can't keep running through this shit. We have to get inside somewhere and rest." He looked the doors up and down. "Maybe this place will do. What is it?"

"Post office," said Jessie, glancing back over Haze's shoulder. The crabs hadn't caught up yet. But how long did they have?

"Maybe we can express mail ourselves the fuck outta here, huh?"

She glared at Damien, who tried a smile on like you try on pants, then let it go. "Then let's get the hell in there and fast. There are five of those fuckers coming after us, and we don't have time to stand here and chit-chat. And we're all out of ammo. Next, we'll be splashing water at them."

"Bet," said Haze, and he handed the Mossberg over to Jessie as he stepped up.

Jessie watched as they exchanged glances, but there were no fireworks. Rick nodded at Haze, and they each grabbed one of the doors and put their backs into it. The doors themselves were about fifteen feet tall, solid wood like barn doors. They groaned when pushed - both the doors and the two men trying to open them. But while the doors were technically open, the space between them wasn't enough to squeeze through, and Jessie's internal alarm clock was going off. She glanced at the corner again, her fingers lingering on her Sig Sauer, wishing she had another clip...or an RPG. A plasma rifle would do in a pinch, too, she decided. They'd be around the corner and on them in no telling how long.

"Fucking help them," she growled, shoving Damien towards the door. "You, too, Muscles. Get your ass over there unless you wanna be next week's crab cake special at Captain James."

"It's Cole," said Muscles, frowning, but he moved.

"I don't care if it's Colleen. Get that fucking door open before those fucking things get around the fucking corner and fucking find us." Jesse stared him down, or stared him up, since she had to crane her neck when he waded past. He was easily six feet tall, which put her eyes in line with his pecs, muscles so swollen they reminded her of her sister and the boob job she'd gotten last year. But his abs were better, she thought for a moment. Then she rolled her eyes and set her mind back on the task at hand. If they could get the doors open even a little, they could squeeze through and close them, maybe find something to lock them from the inside. That would give them some peace and quiet, some time to rest and maybe a chance to survive this whatever the hell it was: a Crabquake?

"Hashtag: fuck this shit." It was Roxie this time. She was watching the four men find a way to work together and pull the doors open, but it was proving difficult. There were no handles or hand grips; the doors were mostly smooth, except for one diagonal cross post, and it was hard to get two people in place on either door to get any real leverage.

"I just want to go home." Jessie glanced at the girl who'd started off her day in a robe and was now in a soaking wet t-shirt and panties and wondered where her home was, if she'd ever see it again. Then the doors creaked and shifted a few inches, bringing Jessie back around.

The doors shifted again and one of them crept open with an angry whine; Muscles, aka Cole, grunted and flexed, and Jessie moved. The hole was big enough to get them through.

"Go! Everyone, go! Inside now." She slammed into Roxie from behind, forcing her forward. Then she turned back to Ashley, and the runners, and the others who all stood around and herded them in like lost cattle. Finally, she pulled Damien and Rick through and stepped past the double set of swinging glass doors into a dark, spacious room flooded almost to her waist. "Rick, get up over the counter and see if we can get upstairs."

He nodded and moved out without a word, and Jessie turned back in time to see Haze and Cole - those muscles had come in handy - step through and pull the doors closed. They were safe for a moment.

<h1 style="text-align:center">13</h1>

"IDRIS ELBA."

"What?" Jessie looked up from wringing out her socks.

"Idris Elba. He played Stringer Bell in The Wire. Dude's badass." Haze leaned back against the wall, taking in Jessie's empty look, trying not to let his eyes wander. She'd been sitting there, her legs dangling over the edge of the table, wringing out her socks for the last few minutes, and he'd tried not to stare. Fail.

"Sorry, I never saw that. I heard it was good."

"Yeah, it was. I mean, I didn't see it when it first came out - we didn't have HBO - we barely had cable some months, but Redbox had all five seasons. So, I got them a couple years ago and couldn't stop watching. It was tight. Stopped after season three though."

He watched her nod as if she understood. He certainly did. Coppin Heights, where his mother still lived, and D for that matter, was all too close to Upton and Harlem Park and all that, those places where drug deals went bad, and cops rolled up and slammed two-bit players up against the hoods of their cars for a little paper and a couple of pills. A little kick, some stick, and them boys was cuffed and pushed down into the back seat of black and white. See ya.

He'd watched Idris intensely - that was the only way he could describe it. The guy was a real actor, and the show really brought out some shit that was close to home, that touched him in ways that he'd wanted to forget. As a kid, he'd been rolling into teenager-hood unsure of his direction, keeping his head down, trying to stay out of trouble. It was hard with Damien always taking the lead. But football had saved him - almost, and then he'd only had one real goal: get the hell out of the hood. Watching everyone die on The Wire, the busts, the backstabbing - it really brought it all home, and made him thankful that he'd gotten out.

Until now. Would he ever be out?

Haze leaned back against the wall and closed his eyes, the black bag behind him acting as a throw pillow. He wanted to watch Jessie wring out her socks a little more, watch her stand and stretch again - what guy didn't? But his eyelids were getting heavy, heavier than his soaked jeans, heavier than his conscience. Heavier than Flaco's badge in his back pocket.

"Oh, he was in that movie with the giant robots, right? And Thor! Yeah, he was cool. A hard ass. Probably too old to play you though, you think?"

When he opened his eyes, Jessie had moved in closer. The socks were nowhere to be seen, and her legs were tucked under her. She was staring at him with a smile on her face, having figured out who Idris was now. She twirled her hair, twisting it up, and then put it into a sort of bun. She finished with a frown, a cute pout that he liked right away.

"I'm gonna need eleven showers and a day at the spa when this is over." She twisted up her face and shrugged. "And my nails. Fuck," she said and tucked her balled up hands under her armpits.

"I think you look sorta hot."

"Jesus. You kidding me? I look like a girl's supposed to look at the end of a disaster movie - like something they dug up from a dark hole. The Walking Dead - you've seen that, right? Only I'm not craving brains; I'm craving a Brillo pad and some industrial soap. Maybe some Old Bay fries from that food truck that comes around on Wednesdays."

"A chicken box. That's what I need right now." Damien plopped down beside them on the dry floor, his sneakers making a squishing sound. "Some chicken and a hot young thing like you, and we're set."

"Watch it, Romeo," mumbled Haze, his lids half closed to the messy refugee camp forming in front of him.

"You two Don Juan's must be desperate. I haven't looked this good since I spent the morning in the bathroom a few weeks ago throwing up all that Fireball. Too much time in prison? I hear it lowers your standards."

Damien cackled. "Mothafuckas can't get me in no jail, baby. I ain't did shit no ways. And Haze, well, he's on the up-and-coming list. Got him a job slinging plates and folded napkins with the white folks; wants to go to culinary art school and be chef. And after this rescue job, mayor's gonna give him a key to the city, ain't that right, dog? Gonna be Haze Day in the Charm City; parades and shit like they do when the Ravens win the Superbowl."

Haze ignored it; just nodded. His eyes were closed again, like it or not, and he didn't have the energy to do anything else. Even when Jessie leaned into him, when he felt her head on his shoulder, he couldn't even wrap her up. He just took a deep breath and said goodnight.

...

The snoring woke him up.

Haze yawned and tried to sit up, but the head in his lap checked his movement. Blonde hair done up in a bun attached to a slender neck poking out of a blue t-shirt - that was the first thing he saw when he opened his eyes. A sudden wave of confusion, and then his brain caught up with his memory, and he yawned again. It wasn't a dream, after all. She was actually there, and that meant all the silly shit he'd been dreaming about had really happened.

They were on the second floor of the Wolfe Street Federal Post Office. There were ten people in the group that had made it that far; a few had been left behind. And out there somewhere were a few, if not dozens or more, massive crustaceans looking for a fight. He scanned the room, listening to the snoring, his eyes lingering over the unmoving shapes that huddled together in what had turned out to be the break room, the only space they could get into without a key besides the lobby downstairs, which was flooded. There were the two runners, older gentlemen snuggled up together in the corner. The muscle guy, his friend who used to own a battered silver beer cooler and the girl who'd been in the pink robe and missing a slipper. They'd come up with some sort of triple spoon maneuver on the floor by the darkened and recently raided soda machine. A half dozen cans of Coke products sat empty on the floor next to them. Rick and Roxie were propped up near the door as far from him and Jessie as possible; that was at least how he read it. Things had changed there. And Damien, he was flat out on the floor on his back, snoring and twitching, probably dreaming of being chased by a giant chicken box with little red legs. D'd had that dream too many times to count, and it never failed to leave Haze laughing when he heard the description again and again.

"What a bunch of fuckups," he mumbled. Fuckups maybe, but they'd survived the morning. His watch and stomach told him it was past lunchtime; his stomach grumbled on cue, confirming it. He swallowed and took another deep breath. Didn't matter; he felt pretty good now. Starving, but good. The knee was still aching, they were still out of ammo, and all they had was a machine half full of room temperature sodas and no food, but they were alive. Oh, and the bathroom worked; that was something.

Not bad for a morning watching the city being destroyed all around them. And despite all the obstacles and threats from the cops and giant crabs and the flood and earthquakes, they still had the money. It was still pay day, and after all this shit, a motherfucker needed to get paid, right?

But that was it, he decided. No more. This bullshit that had gotten him almost arrested, almost killed, and in the middle of a disaster of epic fucking proportions. Not again. His gaze wandered over to his friend, a guy he'd known longer than anyone, and he shook his head. Sometimes mothafuckas just had to go; you had to get them out of your life, no matter how close they were. He had to cut ties. D would understand, wouldn't he? He'd take his cut and walk. It was time to get out of Baltimore.

And it was time to get the hell out of here. Safe or not, they had to get moving. There was nothing for them here before who knows what else happened. No food, no medical facilities, no way to call anyone, and no way to fight the crabs if and when it came down to it again. Where were the cops, the Marines?

"We gots to go," he muttered, and Jessie rolled over, her blue eyes blinking open to meet his.

She swallowed, wiped her mouth with the back of her hand. "Hi."

"Hi." He mirrored her half-smile. "You okay? Sleep okay?"

"Yeah. Good enough. What were you saying?"

"Huh? Oh, I was just talking to myself. We need to get out of here."

Jessie groaned as she sat up, pulling her legs up underneath her on the floor. "So sore. Feels like high school field hockey all over again." She yawned, covering her face with her hands, and pushed a strand of hair out of her eyes. "Yeah, you're right. We can't stay here. That Ashley girl needs medical attention. We need food. You need someone to look at your knee."

Haze nodded, a little disappointed that she'd moved, but happy that she was still only inches away. He watched her intently, thinking that if she looked that good during a disaster, she was a keeper. "We gotta tell someone where to find Flaco."

"And the other cops."

"And that little old lady, Mrs. Whatsitski or whatever."

Jessie giggled. "Swaslowski.

"Yeah. I mean, I don't know what to do, but it seems like the right kinda thing, right?" But hadn't he just decided to take the money and walk?

Jessie yawned again and stretched, then reached for an unopened Sprite nearby. The can cracked open with a snap, and she took a few sips, offered it to Haze, who accepted. "Yeah, it's the right thing to do.

I don't know what you're supposed to do. In movies people just walk away and go do their own thing, and that seems kinda shitty, doesn't it? To just walk away and let it all go?"

"Well, that's the movies, right?"

"Or books. Yeah, it is. But this is neither. We don't just ride off into the sunset. There are people left behind - friends and others that we have some kind of responsibility for, right? Like this ragtag bunch we picked up along the way?"

"I dunno." Haze looked out over the band of misfits. The snoring continued in waves. He took another sip and swallowed, wishing the machine had been on and the soda was still cold. "I guess so." He passed the Sprite back.

"Well, let's get them, and us, the rest of the way out of this mess. Rick had a good idea. We go to Patterson Park where there's high, open ground, and then we'll at least be dry, maybe safe."

"Bet."

Jessie nodded and reached for her socks.

It was time to get moving, and Haze knew where to start.

"Now what?" said Rick when Haze prodded him.

"We're getting outta here. Patterson Park like you said." He squatted; he didn't like looking down on the guy. The situation was already fucked up between them, and it didn't need to get worse. "We can't just sit here and wait for shit outside to get better. We gotta get to high, open ground like you said - no buildings to fall on us or fires to run from. And we got no food here."

"And isn't that girl over there hurt?" Rick sat up and pointed toward the three that Jessie was now waking up.

"Yeah, cut her foot or something." They watched as she examined the makeshift bandage. There wasn't much left of Muscles' shirt now, and what was there on Ashley's foot was stained red. Jessie unwrapped it slowly while Cooler Dude held the girl's hand.

Roxie chimed in as she sat up. "I'm starving, Rick."

"We all hungry, baby." Haze glanced at her, trying to keep his voice in check. His stomach was knotting up, and he wished as much as anyone they'd found a spot to hold up in one of the restaurants that littered Fells Point, but she didn't need to point that shit out.

"Yeah, but my blood sugar is getting low. I can feel it."

Haze looked at her again, then past her to the empty cans of soda that littered their corner. "Diabetic?"

"Type 1. Feeling a little shaky, and I don't have my insulin. It was in my purse."

Fuck. The reasons to get going were stacking up like bodies.

"We're gonna get you outta here, baby. We'll get you somewhere safe and get to the EMTs or someone, okay?" Rick took her hand and squeezed it.

Haze took that as his cue, feeling the ache again. Not just the one in his empty stomach, but the fatigue in his legs and the stiffness in his knee and ankle. It was gonna be a long day, and it was only half done.

He looked back down at Rick. "So, we good?" His eyes darted across the room to Jessie and came back to rest on the newly-exed boyfriend.

Rick's eyes narrowed, and then it seemed to sink in what was going on. "Yeah." He glanced at Jessie - she was wrapping the girl's foot now with another strip of t-shirt - then he looked back. "We're good."

"A'ight. Because we ain't getting far without you. Cool?"

Rick nodded. "It's cool. But..." He hesitated. "Should I talk to her?"

Haze glanced over and back. "You think she wants to talk to you? Why do you think I'm over here now. Clearing the air. Handling this like adults, right? We work as a team to get outta this shit, and then we deal with the fallout. Right now, we gotta survive." Rick nodded. "Get us to Patterson Park, and then we worry about the rest of this bullshit."

"Yeah. Yeah, that's cool."

"Bet. Then let's get rolling. Get Cole and the other dudes up, the runners, and let's get it together. We still need to see if the coast is clear or if it's all crab bisque out there on Wolfe."

"Where's the fucking army?" said Roxie, grumbling as she pushed up and got to her feet.

"I don't know, but we don't have any more ammo. We have nothing to hit them with empty soda cans. We need some industrial strength pepper spray. Got any?"

Roxie shrugged. "I had some in my purse in case some hood..." She paused when she looked up, then licked her lips and her eyes found the floor again. "But I lost that back at the bar. Like that would help anyway."

It had been a joke, but the moment those final words spilled from Roxie's cracked lips, Haze remembered something he'd seen just that morning. The old woman, Mrs. Swaslowski - he finally had the name down, had held off that first crab attack, and she hadn't had a gun or a tank. Haze looked from Roxie to Rick and back again, feeling the virtual light bulb going on over his head.

"So where can we get some?"

"What? Pepper spray?" Roxie popped open another can of orange soda and took down a few swallows before she answered. "You can't. It's a controlled substance. You have to have a permit and get it at an authorized dealer. It was a bitch to get mine, but totally worth it."

"Yeah, I saw someone use it right outside the bar on a creepster," said Rick. "He ran off, and the girl came back in and ordered another drink. I think her ex stalked her down there. She got him, then just tucked it back in her purse and got drunk."

"I remember that. Yeah, it was her ex. Carlos or something." Roxie shrugged. "He was a dick."

Haze nodded. The nostalgia was getting them nowhere, but the concept had a chance. "So, what if I told you that I saw an old woman use pepper spray on one of those big ass crabs and it stopped it cold?"

Blank stares.

"Right back there on Bond Street by your place. Mrs. Swaslowski. Before we could get to her, the crab was on her, but she sprayed it and the fucking thing backed off. They have eyes, you know?"

"So?"

"So, is there anywhere we can get some pepper spray around here?" And when both of them shrugged, Haze went on. "Then what about a substitute? Will real pepper work?"

Rick laughed. "We'll make 'em sneeze to death!"

"Hey, I'm not a fucking chemist. Is there something we could use here or could get somewhere nearby and use as a substitute?"

"How about Old Bay? You know crabs hate that; plus, they'll already be seasoned when we eat 'em." Roxie giggled and jiggled. Haze pretended not to notice any of it, and suddenly he wished she'd just stop talking. He was even about to say so, or at least turn around and walk away - this line of thought was a waste of time, after all, but then Rick spoke up.

"That might just work. The spices in it - I mean, it's just red and black pepper and salt and a few ingredients they don't list, but do you think you want that in your eyes? If we had some, we could dump it in something or pack it in something that might break open when we throw it, like a bomb or something, and that might be enough to hurt one of those things and send them running."

Haze just stared, unsure of what to say. Was this guy for real? Or was he just trying to impress this chick? He'd seen dudes do less, heard them spout out some serious bullshit to get balls deep, but this might take the proverbial cake.

"I know what you're thinking, but really - pepper in your nose makes you sneeze to high Heaven; pepper in your eyes? You wanna take a shot and see how it comes out first? I guarantee you won't like it." Rick stared back, mouth grim and no mocking or laughter in his eyes. He might be full of shit, but he was being real.

"No shit?"

"No shit. And I know just where we can get all we can handle. We just have to get out of here."

14

"SHIT. IT'S FARTHER than I thought."

"What do you mean -," Haze dropped his voice halfway through the sentence, "- it's fucking farther than you thought. This is your hood." He growled through his teeth, then turned away with what Jessie thought was murder in his eyes.

Then all she could do was shake her head. Rick was fucking up again. And this time it might cost them.

Of course, the crabs had been waiting for them, but maybe not waiting so much as standing around outside the post office where they'd been led by their fleeing two-legged food. Apparently, there wasn't any other food around since Jimmy's collapsed, so they'd waited, which meant Jessie and the rest of them had to sneak out the back. The back door of the Wolfe Street Post Office led to a small courtyard/parking lot with only one exit, which was blocked by a seven-foot-high black metal fence. And it wasn't some cheap knock-down, chain link, Dundalk backyard fence; this was a solid, even attractive, solid metal fence with a gate that slid aside when activated. Only there was no activating it, so they'd had to climb it. And that hadn't worked as well as anyone had hoped. In fact, it had been downright comically tragic, or tragically comical, when Damien and Rick had had to basically forklift Roxie over, and the runners did a piss poor job of catching her. Instead of a quiet, subtle move, her scream and the subsequent splashdown, which reminded Jessie of trips to the National Aquarium dolphin show as a child, had alerted the lurkers.

Suddenly the chase was back on.

And of course, that would have only been a huge problem until they hit the corner at Aliceanna Street and she and Rick both realized that the Captain James restaurant, home of the best crab cracking in Southeast B'more, was not one block away, but three blocks away on a street currently being swallowed by gray harbor water. Now it was an ocean-sized problem.

In her defense, Jessie wasn't hitting on all cylinders after the morning they'd had. Who would be?

"Goddamnit, Rick," she muttered, her eyes fixed on the prize.

Jutting out at the corner, where Aliceanna and Boston streets formed an acute angle, the ship-shaped seafood restaurant glimmered in the distance like a massive lifeboat, if not the pointy end of the Titanic. And if they ever got to it, there was a chance at some food and shelter, and an endless supply of Old Bay that they could use to fight back. Until then, if there was a then, they were on their own.

And things weren't looking so good on that front.

Jessie looked back and groaned. They'd had a head start, and a decent one, but it wouldn't last. The reddish-brown shells were coming around the corner already, bobbing like corks but moving along in their own deceptive way. Claws were already snapping. Little beady eyes staring at them just over the tops of the waves. How many? She didn't slow down to count them, but it was obvious there were more than a few. More than they could handle.

Ahead, the rest of the group ran/waded through the waist-high waves. Jessie wrinkled her nose against the foul chemical smell and wondered if it was time to move to somewhere far away from the water. There weren't many floods or giant crabs threatening Kansas City, were there? And in Kansas City she wouldn't have to worry about a half dozen vaccinations at Hopkins later in the week to keep whatever flesh-eating bacteria or bowel-rotting diseases that lived in the harbor from killing her, either. Plus, she'd heard they had good barbecue. But it was Kansas, after all, and that pretty much spelled b-o-r-i-n-g.

The Charm City would have to do, killer crabs and deadly harbor water and all. Greatest City in America! It's what they put on the bus stop benches.

But after this, it was time for a vacation, if she could scrape together the money. Maybe Aruba?

"This way. Hurry." Jessie looked up, blinking out of her reverie and thoughts of crystal-clear water and sand between her toes and drinks with little umbrellas (far away from Woody's). She shrugged and followed as the group jinked left through a chain link fence next to a white two-story building. Before she could even open her mouth to ask what was going on, Haze pulled her through and pushed the tall gate - nothing like the last one, but an obstacle nonetheless - closed. "There's no lock, but I don't think those claws are good for much but smashing and chopping things into pieces."

"Yeah, I think you're right," was all Jessie could muster before Haze had her by the arm again, dragging her forward through the black water. "Where?" But she let it go when she saw Rick leading the way behind the building, and soon they found themselves in a narrow alley parallel to the street. That's when they all came to a standstill.

Both Haze and Rick, as if their minds were linked - had they worked it all out when she wasn't watching? - held fingers up to closed lips, silencing the protests and complaints. And a few seconds later, they were standing in silence up to their waists in rippling waves. "Not a sound," said Haze in a whisper. "We're moving this way. Slow and steady. No splashing. No talking."

He had it together, and he had their attention, even their obedience, for the moment. Even hers, as Jessie shut down the questions that were running through her head.

Behind them she could hear the sloshing, the creepy warbling coming closer, and the hairs stood up on the backs of her arms. Before they'd moved more than a few yards, the gates rattled, and the metal shrieked. "Move," growled Jessie between clenched teeth, and Haze nodded and pushed forward slowly, hands up and palms down to keep everyone calm. Rick echoed his earlier gesture, calling for quiet, and they eased along the alley, leaving the clatter of the gates behind.

Ahead, they waded into what had been a parking lot, a couple of old tractor trailer cabs parked alongside a dark gray building, a few sedans mostly underwater nearby, and a gray-blue flat-bed tow truck. The concrete sloped upwards via a long ramp, and before Jessie knew it, the water had receded to her knees. That brought a sigh of relief, and a little chatter, but it also meant the noise level was up as water sloshed and splashed around them, so the ex slowed them down to a crawl and went into schoolteacher overdrive with his gestures of silence. Jessie almost giggled despite herself watching the ex - was that how she was thinking of Rick already?

She slowed then, watching him, the ex, moving the herd along, watching him take charge in a way that he'd seemed to have in him when they'd first met. Shoulder-length black hair matted to his face, shades of stubble lining his jaw, he was still as sexy as he'd always been and still had that Taylor Kitsch thing going on, but the thing with Roxie - what was she supposed to do? And here was that word popping up in her head: "ex". Just like that, unbidden, it appeared. That had to mean something, didn't it?

On the other side of the group was someone else, the guy who'd appeared out of nowhere, like the "ex" word. He'd swept her off her feet in a way. She giggled again at the thought of it. He'd helped when he didn't have to, taken care of complete strangers, including a policeman who'd at first threatened him, and he'd even risked his life for her. And yet, she didn't even know his real name. Had he even mentioned it, or had it been "Haze" the whole time? She couldn't even remember. He was the guy that smiled when he looked her way, the guy that brought a smile to her lips when she looked at him, and that was good enough for now. Wasn't it?

Jessie watched him, how he maneuvered their crew along, and felt the corners of her mouth turn up, then he looked back and shrugged, and she realized she was falling behind and needed to get going. Their little crowd was rounding the back of the red truck and heading down a ramp now behind the next building, the water creeping back up their legs, a few muffled groans, and a little muttering echoing in the quiet space.

Trying to keep her sloshing to a minimum, Jessie looked behind them along the back alley, but there was nothing. The plan, it seemed, was working. Wasn't it? At least for now. Smart boys; ditch the crabs in the alley. She smiled despite everything around her and what might still be waiting for them ahead. Maybe they'd make it to Captain James, after all, and Old Bay or not - she knew there'd be some, tons, in fact - at least they'd have food. And clean water. And who knew? Maybe even a few gallons of hand sanitizer.

Ahead, the alley ended, opening back on the street, and it was there in the muted shadow of the gray building that they stopped while Haze crept to the edge of the structure and looked out onto Aliceanna Street again. Jessie came up from the rear, skirting the crowd but feeling the nervousness, seeing it in their eyes, the twitchy glances, the fidgeting. They were exposed here, and whatever was after them wasn't all that far off if they'd made it as far as the chain link gate. Give or take fifty yards, she figured. And that only told them what was behind them. She had no idea what was in front.

Then Haze turned around, his mouth twisted into a disappointing look. "They're not that far away. We're going to have to keep on the creep. Slow, steady, hug the buildings and not make a sound."

"We've still got a long way to go."

"Can't think of it like that. We'll just creep, and they won't even know we're there."

"See anything towards Captain James?"

"Looks like maybe something that way, but it's hard to say - water everywhere from the street on out. Shit floating on the water. I can see the tops of cars all in a line and some small boats that must have come loose in the quake. It looks like the marina has moved about a hundred yards inland."

"Crabs?"

"Dunno, but if there are any, they could be underwater, and we wouldn't know it until it was too late. And the ones we already know about will be faster - us slower - where the water's deep."

Jessie shook her head. It was a no-win situation. They couldn't go back, and going forward was a mystery. And so far, no amount of trying to be quiet had really worked. If there were more crabs, what would they do then? They needed a distraction.

"Maybe there's something else that can slow them down, buy us some time?"

Haze shrugged, but Jessie had an idea, and she waved Damien and Rick over and laid it on them.

Damien cackled when he heard the plan, but then he clammed up when he realized he was part of it. "Why me?"

"Because you can hotwire a car." Haze shook his head.

"Not a fucking semi, yo. I ain't no truck driver. See?" He pointed at his head. "No straw hat."

"Well, you are today, Damien. We need you. And I can drive a big truck. My dad was a truck driver. I just might not be able to start it, you gotta come with, okay?" Jessie shifted from serious mode to cute girl mode on the fly, from grumpy frown to smiles and twinkly eyes. She would have twirled her hair if it hadn't been flattened on her head like an old shag carpet. "This is the way we get our friends from here to Captain James safely. It's your turn to be the hero." Then she leaned in close, her lips inches from his ear. "Roxie might think that's hot."

That was enough to seal the deal, and a few moments later, Jessie was slinking back around the building toward the hulking red semi that sat silent in its parking space.

The plan was simple enough: get in the truck, get it started, and make a lot of noise. That would distract everything around them and give the rest of the crew a chance to get down the street. And maybe, if she could get the thing moving - she'd sort of lied about being able to drive it, but not about her dad driving the big rigs - then maybe she could get a little revenge for Flaco and Mrs. Swaslowski. And that last bit made it all worthwhile. It wasn't like some silly crabs could hurt a semi, even ones as big as a Prius.

Jessie scrambled up and pulled herself into the cab on one side while Damien took the other. She flipped the visor, hoping for keys - you never knew; it worked in the movies. But so did stealing cars, and once they were settled in, Damien just stared at the steering shaft.

"So? What's next?"

"Girl, I stole a Honda once. A few Buicks - easy pickings; maybe that's why they don't make 'em anymore. And Camrys? Piece of cake if you got the tools, but damn, this? I was hoping the keys would be in it."

Jessie just stared at him, suddenly deflated. What would they do now? Just swim for it? Just drag a few hurt, scared and hungry people two blocks before they get eaten? What kind of heroes were they now? Just running. Just tired. Just nobody. Just like always.

She sighed. "Gig's up. Let's get the flock out of here then."

Damien shrugged. "Sorry, sistah, just don't got the skills you need for this kinda thing. And no tools. This ain't the movies, you know?"

"Yeah," Jessie said and took one last look at the cab. She giggled, feeling the odd moment of nostalgia, remembering her dad and his big rig. And then the giggle burst into full blown laughter when she popped open the center console near the gear shift. A shard of silver gleamed in the low light, and Jessie reached in and grabbed the keys. "Just where Daddy left his."

"Da fuck?" Damien's eyes lit up when he heard the jingle of keys. "We're in business."

Jessie nodded, a big grin stealing over her face as she swiveled around to the steering wheel and dashboard. Now if she could only remember how to start the damned thing up. The biggest key on the ring slid easily into its slot, and she stretched to reach the gas and clutch; the cab wasn't built for a little thing like her in mind. She'd need a pillow or phone book or - she shrugged off her backpack and let it drop into place behind her butt, pushing her forward a bit. Perfect. Only she needed something bigger and immediately eyed Damien.

"I need your bag, D. Right back here behind me so I can sit up." She waited, watched him stare back, then let out an exasperated gasp. "So, what the fuck, D? Gimme your bag. Got some sweaty drawers you can't do without? Spank sock?"

He seemed to snap into motion the moment she snapped her fingers, then slid the bag off his shoulders and handed it over with a grim look on his face, all close mouthed and eyes staring at the seat. "Sorry. No problem."

"Thanks," she said with a toothless smile and a little attitude. "Now let's get this show on the road."

They exchanged glances, and she turned the key, her stomach alive with butterflies.

The engine rumbled, shaking the whole cab, then it died just as quickly. Jessie frowned but turned the key again. Rumble; die. And again; same result. "All talk; no action - just like a guy," she muttered and didn't care if Damien heard. They needed more than that, and they needed it fast. Jessie glanced out the window, checked her mirrors. Nothing yet. Yet. The crabs would come to the noise sooner or later, but if they didn't get the damn truck going, she and Damien were getting nowhere fast, and how the hell would they get out of the cab?

"Hit the gas, girl. Get this thing started."

"It's not that easy. It's not a Buick." Jessie wouldn't even look at him. She could see his eyes without having to look up, hear the frustration in his voice, the anger. But she couldn't just keep cranking on the key and hoping for the best. There was something more to it. She was sure. But what was it?

"Come on. Come...oh shit." Jessie didn't have to look up; Damien's voice said it all.

"Fuck."

"Fuck is right, homegirl. Let's get this mothafucka right. Start her up already!" He practically bounced in his seat. "They coming!"

But Jessie didn't have to look up to know that either. She felt the truck shimmy as the waves hit it, then the warbling hit her ears. She stared at the steering wheel, past it to the dash. It was an older truck she'd learned on, but this one should operate the same way, right? And what had her Daddy shown her then? She closed her eyes to try and picture him in the cab, the bright red seats and the dashboard lit up like a Christmas tree. And then the whole cab shook as the first massive claw struck her door.

"Fuck fuck fuck fuck fuck! Let's go, Jessie! God damnit! Get that shit in gear, girl!"

That was it! She laughed out loud, cackling like a crazy person or one of the homeless shuffling down Fleet Street after hours. Daddy had always left the truck in first gear so it wouldn't start right away - just in case someone wanted to drive off with his baby and the custom paint job while he was grabbing a quick T-bone or a cup of coffee and a donut. That was what the truckers at the truck stops did from Maine to California, and just like them, when she pumped the clutch and smacked the gear shift, it popped out of first and into neutral just as she turned the key. The dash lit up just as another massive claw rocked the driver's side door.

"Go! Go! Go! Go!"

Jessie glared at Damien. "Shut the fuck up already!" Then she double-checked the gauges, turned the key, and hit the gas. The engine growled and then rumbled to life, drowning out the warbling, Damien's hooting, and her own hysterical laughing. Then, as the engine noise died down to a low roar, she slammed the truck into reverse.

"Let's make some crabby patties," she screamed, and hit the gas.

15

THE MOMENT HE HEARD the truck's engine roll over and come to life, Haze motioned for them to go.

"Move your asses," he said, voice just above a whisper. "Fast and quiet. Just like we said." And they did, Rick leading the way with Roxie in tow. He wouldn't stray five feet from her, which Haze didn't get. He'd spoken with, worked with and run with Jessie, watched her shoot, even kissed her, and every time he looked at Rick all up on Roxie's helpless ass, the only thing he could do was shrug. Some things never made sense. But for once, Rick had made some sense. It'd been his idea to go behind the buildings on Aliceanna and hide from the crabs, and that had bought them some time and Rick a reprieve from being a total loser...so far.

Meanwhile, his boy and his - he stopped and wondered for a second, looking back - was Jessie his girl now? It was probably a little too early for all that, he decided. Whatever she was, she and D were behind them now trying to get that truck moving, trying to give them a chance. It had given them a couple of false starts, had Haze pushing the crew back every time the truck died, but now it both sounded and looked like things were a go.

He eased down the flooded sidewalk, moving as slowly as he could to stay quiet, all while trying to give his aching knee a break and look back. He'd seen the crabs near the gate; just like back at the post office, they'd just stood there like dumb animals, like drunks waiting for the corner bar to open again, swaying on unsteady legs, desperate for their fix. The doors opened - in this case, the truck roared to life -

and suddenly they were shambling, drooling winos headed for the bar. Only this bar had a hefty cover charge.

With a flash and a crash, the bright red cab backed out over the top of another section of chain link fence, throwing a fountain of water into the faces of the onrushing mob. Crabs tumbled in every direction, scattered by the force of the truck and the cascading waves, as the truck whirled, tilted and almost toppled over in the middle of the street. Haze cringed until the truck bounced solidly back on all six wheels. He could see the dirty blonde hair in the window and imagined the Cheshire Cat-like grin on Jessie's face as she turned the massive wheel and gunned the engine. Or maybe it was terror - there was no way to know. Black smoke belched from the twin stacks as the truck plowed into the waist-high harbor water, banging into red shells, sending the cranky crustaceans careening across the waves and into the automotive wrecks that now lined Aliceanna Street, er, Canal.

Haze turned away from the crabby calamity just as he heard the semi's horn blare out across the waves. It was the "go" sign he'd been waiting for, even though no one had waited.

"They'll be alright," he muttered to no one. The rest of the group was a dozen yards ahead by now, and he grumbled to himself as he picked up the pace, using his hands as paddles to propel himself along as quickly and quietly as possible past low-slung storefronts and rowhomes that looked like they'd seen better days.

It took no time to catch them, whether the boys up front were being extra cautious, or they were just taking their sweet time. Haze gritted his teeth and kept silent. He couldn't press them if he wanted, not with the shooting pain in his knee. All he could do was focus on what was ahead, take it one step at a time. He caught himself smiling, silently laughing at himself as he heard his coach's voice, heard his own voice in post-game interview after post-game interview. They'd take it one game at a time, one practice at a time, one drill at a time. One step at a time, and try not to think about the pain, something else he'd learned to do. But that was a while ago.

Their progress was glacial, and as much as that helped with his aching knee, it also gave Haze time to turn and watch the shenanigans behind him. Looking back, he had to admit seeing the truck jinking left and right across the street as they exacted a little revenge on some future meals was the dumbest shit he'd ever seen. He laughed and pushed ahead, stealing glances back with every metal-on-metal grind and every blast of that air horn. The semi cab careening down the street in the other direction reminded him of those old slip-n-slide commercials he'd seen on TV; little white kids in neighborhoods with yards no bigger than a chicken strip running and sliding down that orange plastic. It looked like the coolest shit he'd never get to do himself. Instead, all they ever had was someone busting open the hydrant on the corner; this was as close as he'd ever been to a water park, so he glanced back when he wanted; the others could just shut the fuck up and get to wading. There was no doubt in his mind that Damien was pissing himself laughing - not like they'd be able to call him on it anyway as wet as everyone was. When he looked back, the cab was barreling down Aliceanna toward them again, having picked up some speed despite water that nearly drowned the tires. The hood was crumpled and scratched - he could see it even from his more distant viewpoint, but after everything it had been through in the past few minutes, it was holding up well. And if Jessie took her time and didn't get too crazy, this would go smooth.

Haze winced as his foot came down on the sidewalk wrong, felt spikes of pain shooting through his thigh. He swallowed his cry and stumbled, tiptoeing forward to keep the weight off the offended limb until two pairs of hands reached up and grabbed him. Then shoulders slipped under his arms, and suddenly the pressure was gone, but not the sting.

"Thanks, fellas," said Haze, grimacing but nodding to the runners.

"No problem, bud," said Mike, his scratchy voice making Haze swallow. "You've been carrying too much of the load yourself."

"Too long," said Marty. "We gotta step up if we're gonna get out of here, right?"

"Bet. My boy's back there doing his shit, too. 'No team, no win' - that's what coach used to say."

"Ball player?"

Haze nodded. "That's how I got this knee."

"Football or futbol?" Marty asked, and for the first time Haze noted a little something that wasn't Bawlmer in his voice.

"You're not from around here."

"Very observant, although I'd thought that my accent was well worn off by now."

"Nobody says 'futbol' around here." Haze attempted to mimic the gentleman supporting his right arm. "We got soccer here."

"Yes, soccer. Well, old habits, mate, or should I say 'buddy', 'pal', 'hon'?" He chuckled after his attempt at Bawlmerese. "I've been here for quite some time - not long after I met Mike when I came across the water on business. Seventy-three it was - entirely too much polyester back in those days for the sweltering summer heat in Bawlmer." He ticked off the last word with all the lack of style and panache of a Baltimorean, smiled and winked. "Almost went right back."

"Yeah, some damn hot summers here, armpits dripping and no AC, but the place grows on you. More people here every day, money, too. Lot of changes before. Now, I don't know..."

Looking up, Haze eyed the other four slogging in front of them, then gazed past them to the row of identical homes leading the way one after the other to their destination. Even though they could no longer see the sidewalk or the asphalt of Aliceanna, he could see that the entire street had shifted, some of the homes leaning in, looming over the sidewalk. He walked the street ahead with his eyes, noting how the once straight arrow seemed to curve to the right here, then walk back left farther down. He'd been here just more than twenty years - never left the city once - and he'd seen how things had changed. And here, slogging through a disaster that smelled of fish and fire and smoke, was a reminder of how things had changed in Baltimore again and what had started all of it: the series of quakes that had split open the asphalt and decimated the construction site, taken down the little rowhome tavern Jessie called home, killed a little old woman right in front of him and flooded what had once been high-end Baltimore turf, prime waterfront property that brought Yuppies and tourists flocking in with their SUVs and big screen TVs and purse-sized pets. And money. Where would they go now?

Where would he?

From where he waded, wincing at the chaffing between his football thighs again, Haze had a clear view of the harbor all the way across to Tide Point. Boats still bobbed in the marina, but now many of them seemed to float at anchor, the wooden docks between them all but sunk under the gray waves. Some of the smaller boats were nothing more than masts sticking out of the water to mark their graves.

Fitting, he thought. It was that kind of fucked up day, after all. He felt the tug of the black bag's straps on his shoulders and wondered if he shouldn't have just stayed in bed, after all. But there was the seed money, right? He just needed to get through to the other side.

But there was no way to tell what was ahead and waiting for them. For him. If nothing else, it was more dangerous this way than the way they'd come. Haze could see the danger back on Wolfe and Lancaster - there was nowhere for it to hide, but here on Aliceanna he was already feeling a deep dread creeping into his bones.

They'd only gotten halfway to their destination and already their cover was fading. No more trees ahead, and while on the left there was a pretty steady show of houses, most of them still standing and accessible, on the right the last building on Aliceanna, a one-level warehouse that had fallen in on itself, gave way to a flooded parking lot and then opened up to the water and an ocean of bobbing boats and flotsam that looked less than inviting. Behind them, the rumble of the truck continued, but fading now. With someone under each shoulder, all he had was his ears, and they told him the distraction they needed here was far behind, too. And people he could count on falling far behind with it. And his knee - he wouldn't be running at any NFL Combines soon.

Out near where the first boat tugged against its mooring, a piece of flotsam shifted instead of bobbed. Haze swallowed. If they weren't in deep enough, shit was about to get deeper.

"We ain't gonna get there like this," he muttered, then he spoke up. "Rick. Yo. Hold up, dog."

Rick slowed, then stopped and turned around, shaking his head. Understanding and exhaustion clouded his eyes. He looked around, scanning the area in the shadow of a three-story rowhome that doubled as a business. The sign read "Charm City Imports", and Haze wished they'd had a boat tied up outside for some exports.

"We got about a block to go, man. It's right there." Rick leaned against the brick, blew out a long breath that still smelled of tequila. He poked a casual finger down the street at the jutting boat shape. "We gotta keep going."

"Shit's not happening, man," said Haze and he nodded out towards the water. "Somebody shit in the pool."

"What?" The look on Rick's face was priceless, but when he followed Haze's eyes, his mouth dropped open, and he squared his back to the bricks. "Fuck. Is that what I think it is?" He pointed out towards the marina and some heads turned.

There, mixed in with the bobbing boats and half-sunken hulks, a few reddish-brown hulls slipped through the waves, growing in size as they came closer. Haze watched them come out of the fog, eyed the others staring mesmerized at the approaching menace as if they were the fabled Four Horses of the Apocalypse or a posse of hood rats come to the good neighborhoods to knock over a couple fat rich kids for cash and cells. The waves cascaded over the shells of the encroaching crustaceans just where the water should have ended and the sidewalk should have begun, then it fell away in rivulets as the creatures came *ashore*, button-like black eyes peeking up over the frothy whitecaps.

"What do we do?" Roxie squealed, then finding Rick with her outstretched hand, she spooned into his thin frame as if she was the missing puzzle piece.

Rick let out a breath that said everything, closed his eyes.

"We need our truck."

"I don't know what we need," said Mike, "but we need it now. Now."

Haze gazed back out across the water. They were about fifty yards away and floating on the tide now, claws submerged but there all the same. For the moment there was nothing to draw them in, but that was about to change.

Down the street, the cab went spinning around in the middle of Aliceanna again and came to rest in the middle of the street. The wholesale destruction around it included more than the crabs that milled around as if they'd just shot up a little West Side heroine. Cars on either side of what used to be the street were smashed and knocked around so much, Haze couldn't even tell exactly where the asphalt ended and the sidewalk began. The truck sat, rumbling, belching black smoke in little angry puffs like a miniature dragon waiting on another knight in shining armor to challenge it. And that meant it was time to call in the reinforcements. What needed done was done, and he didn't know how much longer they had.

"Time to go, dog."

"Okay," said Rick, and he pushed through the small crowd, wading out a bit into the street. He cast one more glance over at the oncoming crustaceans and put his fingers in his mouth. A shrill whistle rang out across the harbor like a ship's horn in the persistent fog.

In answer, the truck blared its air horn and the engine rumbled.

"Now look sharp," said Haze, looking back at the crabs orienting on the sound and movement. "Company's coming. Let's fucking move. Run!"

They ran. Swam. Waded. Whatever it was, it reminded Haze of the beach scenes early in that old movie Jaws. They moved through the water like only scared people could. It was haphazard. It was slow, but it was progress, and they still had a city block to go.

Haze could hear the semi coming now, hear the spray from the fenders, the growl of the massive engine sitting high and dry a few feet above the water. It'd been a good call, he thought, having them distract the crabs, do a little demolition derby with them, and maybe give the rest of the crew time to get away. But there'd always been the unknown to contend with, and so they'd set up the signal. If they got into trouble, he'd fire the shot and the cavalry would come. If the truck held up and didn't flood. If there was enough fuel in the thing to pull off the bumper cars plan. If the crabs weren't too big. And so far that was the case - it was all working out. So far.

"On the truck," he yelled as the battered behemoth caught up to them. He ducked into the spray, ignored the cursing from the others, and moved to the back of the cab where it flattened out and hooked to the trailers it might one day pull again. For now, it was his ark, and once the truck slowed, Haze pushed bodies up on the back, two-by-two, until they were all tenuously loaded, holding on to whatever they could grab. Then he leaped up onto the running board and grabbed the side mirror. "Let's go!"

Jessie gunned the engine again, almost drowning out the screams in back. Haze slipped as he turned, but caught himself, his foot dangling inches above the murk. He groaned but held on, watched the massive crabs almost on them, reaching wildly with claws the size of his grandma's kitchen table. Now there was nothing but the speed of the truck in waist-high water, and he shook his head as he watched them gain a little bit of an edge. It probably wasn't going to be enough. The truck was too slow, the crabs too fast, the water too deep.

Maybe, he thought to himself and peeked back in the direction they were moving. Maybe. Captain James was closer, closer than he ever thought it would be. They would have to get up on the roof, the second story, as Rick had mentioned. There was a blue awning over the back door they could use to get up there; that would get them out of the water, and there was a door up there the owners used to put out Christmas lights and other decorations. They'd figure out how to get in once they got there.

Crumbling houses and another oceanic parking lot passed by on the left at a speed that made Haze itch, but before he knew it, they were crossing over Chester Street and the big boat-shaped restaurant, massive blue awning and second story railing that made the place look like an old steam liner, was right there. He heard Jessie downshift and he pulled himself in close as Jessie maneuvered the truck up onto the sidewalk and tight against the building. Then the engine rumbled and went silent. "Move your asses," he barked and scrambled around to the back end, watching out for moving bodies, his eyes drifting back to the pursuit. Claws waving, water dripping off them like they were salivating, the monstrous crabs were coming on fast.

"Go, go, go!"

Haze turned to watch Mike and Marty scramble up onto the roof of the cab. Muscles, aka Cole, was already helping Ashley over to the awning. He tested the weight, shook his head, and leaped, massive meat hooks snagging the lower rungs of the railing. They groaned, but held, and he executed a clean pull-up until he had a foot in place and his elbow hooked over the top of the railing. "Come on," he said, free hand reaching down, and he pulled her up like she was made of paper. Then he reached for the next guy.

Haze nodded, feeling like it might work, as Jessie scrambled up out of the cab and joined him. "Move your ass." She opened her mouth to say something, but he grabbed her and propelled her up onto the cab. "Got no time for words now, girl."

Rick was next, with Roxie right behind him, Damien, of course, volunteered to stay below and push. He had both his mitts on the flesh that flowed from her short-shorts and a shit-eating grin on his face despite the effort, but with Rick's help, and a lot of unnecessary squirming on Roxie's part, not to mention her constant wailing about the closing crabs, they got her up on the cab and across to the restaurant. Haze pulled himself up behind Damien and shoved him toward Muscles as Rick went across. "We're off this bitch," he said and looked back just as the first crab crashed into the truck, sending him and Damien careening over the edge.

16

SCREAMS BATTERED JESSIE'S ears; she wasn't sure if one of them was hers or not just then. All she knew was Haze and Damien were in the water and there were crabs closing in all around them. But what was she supposed to do? They had no weapons, and harsh words and screaming wasn't going to get the job done. They needed something; they needed to do something.

"Rick!" She turned on him, pulling him away from the railing, where he and the others gawked. "The Old Bay. Now. Move it."

Why else had they come here but for the damned spice? As if it would actually work! She'd been skeptical, but Rick had an idea, and somehow it seemed reasonable. She'd shrugged; she'd had nothing else to offer, so maybe it would work. But to be honest, she thought as she drug the ex-boyfriend over to the blue door with the center porthole, she hadn't been sure they'd get far enough to test the theory. But now, it was gonna happen. Because, if they didn't make it work - she didn't want to think about it.

Pulling her Sig from its holster, she pivoted the business end around and put the full power of her high school tennis backhand into it. The glass shattered with the first strike, and the dangling edges dropped away with the added taps of the gun's butt. It had always worked in the movies, and it seemed like real life followed suit. When Jessie reached through, she flipped the lock and opened the door to a small black space, rounded on one side and lined with curtained windows. The other side led to a staircase, and she grabbed Rick's hand and pulled him down.

"Do something, Rick. And fast." Behind her, Jessie could hear the rest of them yelling from their perches upstairs; she tried to shut it out.

"The kitchen," he said, already in motion.

They dove down the stairs and hit the main floor, a triangular sort of room lined with rough-hewn wooden tables still in neat rows - probably bolted to the floor, but the plastic chairs had been tossed in every direction and lay in a few inches of dark water. The muted natural light of the foggy afternoon poured in from wide portholes that lined both walls like eyes, casting an eerie pall over the empty place and its assorted jetsam.

Jessie shuddered. Something about the place reminded her of a cemetery, each table a headstone to a thousand little creatures that were getting their revenge right outside. Ironic, wasn't it?

"Move," said Rick, tapping her shoulder and pulling her out of her own head.

Jessie jumped despite herself and moved on, looking the place up and down, not seeing anything that might resemble a weapon. Rick wasn't waiting. He was already halfway to the other end, zigzagging through debris and only a few steps from a pair of metal doors. "This way," he called, and then he was gone, leaving the doors swinging in slow motion through the ankle-deep flood waters.

And steeling herself, she moved out in long, impatient strides.

Rick was banging around when she got through to the kitchen. She felt around near the frame, found the lights and flicked them on. Only nothing happened, and a dozen curses bottled up against her closed lips. From out of the blackness, she heard a bang, followed a stanza of melodic profanity reflected back at her - something about a cast iron pan. Then the banging resumed, and Jessie followed the noise, hands outstretched. Around the corner, behind a half wall, she found a series of shadows that had to be deep friers, and just past that she encountered a half-lit vision of Rick, muted light pouring through another porthole and illuminating his raised arm. He swung down with the massive cast iron pan, and another clang rang out, accompanied by a flurry of cuss words.

"What are you doing?"

"I dunno," said Ricky, turning and brandishing the pan like a weapon. "Breaking into what looks like a storage cabinet. Maybe there's Old Bay in here, and then we have to mix it with something."

"We don't fucking have time for that, Rick." She could still hear the yells from outside, then suddenly, as if in response to her statement, something hit the outer wall of the kitchen hard. "Fuck, we gotta get them outta there now."

Rick whirled, his eyes in shadow as the light played across the right side of his face. "And how do you fucking propose to do that?"

The words "I don't know" lingered on the tip of Jessie's tongue, and she felt the breath leaving her lungs, breath that would give those words life and dash the hope that she was still clinging to. Only just before that moment came, something snapped into place, and she realized that had seen weapons, ones that would work in a pinch. The words just poured out as the idea formed, some part of her brain working in overdrive and formulating the idea out of thin air. "Fire extinguisher. And a few bottles of vodka."

The outer wall thudded again, showering them with dust from above.

"If we don't have time to get the Old Bay, we sure as fuck don't have time for party tricks."

"Yeah, we do. Now get your ass out there and get me three bottles of something - vodka, gin, how about some Rumchata? Whatever's not broken. Grab some of those cloth napkins from the bar and some matches. I'm getting the fire extinguisher, and then we're going out the side door and do it up right."

"Rescue time?"

"Only this rescue won't require shot glasses. After, maybe, but not right now. Got it?"

Jessie could see Rick's face turn up in a smile, or half of it anyway, and it reflected hers. It was a plan - a good one even, if it worked. If it didn't, well, she could always say she'd finally been to Captain James and tried the crabs.

"Aye, Captain," he said, and he was gone.

In the dark, it was hard to get the extinguisher off the wall. Time seemed to drag, and she wondered as she lugged it up and set it on the counter next to the kitchen door how long they'd been in the restaurant. It seemed like minutes, minutes that seemed like hours, hours that seemed like an eternity. She could hear the screams again now that she was back in the dining room, hear some sort of commotion outside, the muffled warbling of the crabs, someone yelling down from the second floor, a cacophony of clanking and thuds just the other side of the wall she was facing. There was either a war going on outside or a sporting event; there was no way to be sure.

"Jesus, Rick..." she started, and then he was by her side again, his arms full of bottles.

"Ready. I have Jim Beam, a couple of rail vodkas, Fireball because it had me throwing up all day one Sunday - remember? - and of course, Rumchata, your drink of choice."

Jessie wrinkled her nose, even though what she was seeing made her want to smile. "Alright, bar's open. Molotov cocktails on happy hour special," she said with a practiced voice. "Get the matches ready, follow me. I'll use the extinguisher if any of them get too close. You light and throw at anything that moves...anything with eight legs, that is."

"Aye, Captain. And if we do this right, I get the claw meat. You know I love the claws."

Jessie laughed and twisted the locks on the side door, then she swung the extinguisher down and gripped the nozzle like a weapon. "Let's go," she growled and hit the artificial wood with her shoulder, feeling the resistance of the water outside, and then it gave way, as if the building was pressurized, and the door swung open while water and the early afternoon gloom poured in.

They came out on the street in front of the cab, and Jessie looked up at two faces in the truck's windshield. They smiled and waved, then the waving turned to frantic gestures, and she spun, bringing up the nozzle and squeezing off a blast of frosty CO2, catching certain death straight in the kisser. The monster warbled in protest and backed away, claws swinging, one of them crashing against the red truck and snapping off the side mirror. The angry growl that belched from Jessie's own mouth scared her a little, but she squeezed the trigger again and gave the fitful crab another sub-zero dose. Then she heard Rick and his familiar cackle behind her, then his voice just as she saw the first bottle of cheap vodka fly over her head.

"Drinks on the house," he roared.

The bottle arched overhead trailing a flame like a falling star, then it hit the massive shell and exploded into a ball of fire to the sound of applause and cheering. Jessie cringed, blinking as the light crashed against her eyes. It was like seeing a miniature sun up close, and for a moment, all she could see was spots before her eyes. She blinked, trying to clear them away, holding the nozzle up at the ready, just in case, but when her vision cleared, the first thing she saw was Haze. She blinked to make the illusion go away, but he was still there a few seconds later, dark eyes, big grin on his face flashing white teeth. And Damien was climbing down out of the cab, a nervous smile on his face.

"Let's get inside, Jessie. You done good," said Haze with a smile, and he grabbed her shoulders and she let him spin her around. They pushed past Rick, who seemed frozen to the spot, watching them, and then they were through the door...for a moment. But before Jessie could even drop the fire extinguisher and turn around, revealing the relieved smile that cascaded across her face, before she could flop down into the nearest chair and give her wobbly legs a break, her job done, and focus on what in this place was edible, she heard Rick's excited voice.

"Where the fuck you going, Damien?"

"D!" It was Haze, and Jessie heard the shock and fear in his words. When she swung around, there were only three of them in the flooding dining room, and the door was still wide open.

"What the...?" The rest didn't matter. She already knew it. Damien had gone back out the door, and they were going after him.

They moved in unison, as if they'd worked out a plan or spent years training together. It just happened like that. Rick handed Haze two bottles, one of them the flat, white Rumchata bottle, and they stepped out into the gloom again. Jessie was right behind them, lugging the extinguisher, nozzle up and ready. It was getting heavier, or she was getting more tired, or both. Beyond the door, the stench from the burning crab hit her in the face, almost doubling her over in a fit of coughing. The carcass floated a few yards away in the middle of the street, unmoving and blackened like a car-sized charcoal briquette, wisps of gray smoke wafting into the air.

"D, get the fuck outta there," yelled Haze, and that's when Jessie saw him, back in the cab.

"The fuck's he doing?" Hadn't they just risked their lives to get him out of the truck a few seconds ago? Did he have a death wish? Did he just want to blow the horn again or use the cigarette lighter?

Just then crabs came out of nowhere, warbling as they swooped around from behind the truck.

"Move, you sorry fuck!" yelled Haze and he lit the Rumchata and flung it. The closest crab burst into a ball of fire and screamed, swerving randomly away, its shell popping like microwave popcorn. But before anyone could move, another two took its place, and this time Rick's aim was a little high. The bottle splashed impotently into the water and the crabs kept coming. The closest one slammed into the truck, its claw coming around and crashing into the cab's passenger door. The metal buckled with an angry whine, then it groaned as the claw landed again. The second crab whipped around the first like lightning in the water, its button-like eyes seemingly fixed on the three morsels that stood outside the famous Baltimore crab shack as if revenge was on its mind.

This time Jessie stepped up. The clawed killers were too close for another firebomb - too close to them and too close to the truck. She aimed and fired with a guttural growl, feeling a little fire in her belly like she often did when she and Rick played Soldier 3 on his PlayStation. The crab hesitated, claws flailing wildly, but it kept coming forward, forcing them back, until Jessie was standing in the doorway again, the white frost from her personal firearm petering out until there was nothing.

Then she dropped the silver canister and stepped back through the door.

"To the roof!"

Before Jessie could even react, Haze was splashing through the room after Rick. She turned and ran, ignoring the massive shape crashing against the open doorway.

At the top of the steps, glass from the broken window crunched under her feet, and once through the door, she found a bunch of backs turned and leaning over the railing, heard the voices again, this time all of them full of fear. Rick stepped back and tossed a Molotov, and the squarish Jim Beam bottle flew through the air like a grenade. His aim was true this time, and the bottle hit the crab nearest the cab. It exploded to a round of cheers.

"Back off, motherfuckers!"

"Somebody get me some Old Bay!"

"D, get out!" Haze yelled as Jessie joined him and leaned over the white railing.

Below, the burning crab twirled like a flaming top, claws flailing against the truck's cab. The other crab still lingered below at the doorway, but just past the truck, several reddish hulks moved in, attracted by the ruckus.

"Rick! More firebombs," said Jessie, and he was off like a shot, pulling Cooler Guy with him.

On the other side of the truck, Damien squeezed out of the broken window next to the wall, a black bag hanging from his free hand. "Got 'em, Haze. Catch!" he yelled and hurled the bag up. It flew, just barely making the top railing, and Jessie snagged it with an outstretched arm. Then Damien disappeared into the cab again and reappeared just as two more crabs joined the party. "Here we go again," he yelled and tossed the other bag just as the nearest crab smashed the truck with both claws.

The bag arched through the air off-target, just out of Jessie's reach. But Roxie reached out and caught it, then went right over the edge. Her scream was interrupted as was her fall when Muscles, faster than Jessie thought possible, snagged the shoulder strap, and held on, gritting his teeth, every muscle in his torso flexing.

Roxie screamed again, dangling in midair with just one hand clutching the other end of the shoulder strap. Below her, the lone crab shifted its focus and raised its claw.

"No!"

Jessie's eyes flipped back to the cab, following the voice, just in time to see Damien gather himself on the roof of the cab and jump. She screamed and leaned over the rail to catch him, but he wasn't jumping across to the awning or the railing like they all did before. He wasn't saving his own ass. He had another destination in mind, and Jessie watched, unable to do anything as he landed on the crab with a blood-curdling scream and slammed both fists down on the iron-like shell.

"D!"

But it was too late. The crab whirled, claws flailing to find the new threat, and Damien somersaulted through the air just as the crab's claw struck Roxie, sending them both splashing down at the creature's feet.

Then the world went silent again as everyone stared. Jessie tried to shut her eyes, wished she was unable to watch, her scream frozen in her throat. She and Rick had risked their lives to save Damien, and he'd thrown it away, but for what? She couldn't turn away from the scene, but stood transfixed, watching it all through the gaps between her fingers, tears streaming from her eyes, the crab still burning, the truck bent and broken and pressed up against the building, and the other monster smashing its claws down into the water onto people she'd once known while the water went red. Behind her, the black bag she'd caught sat on the deck where she'd dropped it. And a few feet away, the other bag, identical to this one, dangled from Muscles' massive paw.

She'd seen enough.

She snatched both bags, throwing them over her shoulder. Her own backpack had come up with her, but she could have done without it. These ones, it seemed, were way more important. They had been to Damien. She felt Haze's eyes on her as she pushed through the door again, but she wouldn't meet them. She needed a drink now, and a chair, and something to eat. Fuck the crabs and the truck and...

When she hit the first floor, splashing through the water that was up to her thighs now, she ignored the footsteps behind her and made straight for the bar, right past Rick and Cooler Guy, both staring at her with bottles and napkins in their hands. A bottle of Jose stared back at her from its spot mid-shelf. How it'd managed to stay upright wasn't important, only that it was there. She pulled it down with professional care, spun the cap off and pressed it to her lips.

The tequila burned her throat, but in the good way she'd learned to appreciate, even love, over the years. But it wasn't the Jose Cuervo that had her looking through tears when she turned around. Haze was there alone, sitting with the matching black bag on the bar. He just stared, his eyes on hers, and waited.

"What's in the bags, Haze?" said Jesse, wiping her eyes. Then, she reached over and set up two shot glasses. "Why did Damien have to die?"

17

HAZE WOKE UP, BACK stiff from the way he was sitting. The room was dark still, and quiet, not a sound from any direction, as if he were the only person in the whole world. He yawned, feeling the deep exhaustion lingering. However long he'd been sleeping, it hadn't been long enough. But it was something, and if the others were smart, they'd found a place to sleep, too. It had been a long morning, and it promised to be a longer afternoon before this *crabquake*, or whatever they wanted to call it, was over.

He winced when he turned his neck, decided against it and leaned back, his eyes resting on the curtain of shadow that hid the ceiling of the Captain James restaurant's kitchen. Out of the corner of his eye, he could see faded gray light slipping through the dirty porthole near the back door. It fell on an array of deep fat fryers next to the freezer door, barely shedding any light on the room at all. And by the brightness, or lack thereof, he had no idea what time it was or how long they'd been asleep. It was the same dead light he'd seen all day, and it'd been the last thing he remembered seeing before passing out.

What a fucking day, he thought. Everything he'd tried to be and do was totally undone. And even his best friend gone. And for what? A little seed money. Some cash they had no business with, damn sure no business stealing. And a dead man on top of it. Even if he hadn't pulled the trigger, he was still part of it, right? Or had Damien paid for it now and everything was square? Or could it ever be square? He'd felt guilty from the get-go, since they walked out of that trailer, but he'd tried to make up for it, hadn't he? There was Jessie and her friends, even if the friends didn't make it. He'd tried. And Flaco. He'd tried. And even

158

Jessie - she was the only success he'd had all day. Saved her twice, and she'd saved his ass, too. Twice even. But was that enough to make up for what went down before?

Haze closed his eyes and saw the flash of the pistol, heard the bang, and he watched the company man in the trailer go down. That was no way to go. Killed by a couple of punks - and what else could he call it? Shit was true. Dude was dead; killed by a stick-up kid from the West Side, and his boy, who had tried to make good and only ended up back in the shit.

"You can take the nigga out the hood, but you can't take the hood out the nigga," he muttered under his breath, and Jessie stirred.

"Hmmm?" Her head was nestled in his lap, her body next to his on the metal prep counters in the far corner of the kitchen.

He looked down on her solemn face, eyes closed under a runaway lock of dirty blonde. Then he eyed the empty Jose Cuervo bottle an arm's length away. The shot glasses were next to it, both upside down, a little ring of tequila still puddled around the rims.

"Nothing." He watched her nod, eyes still closed. "Nothing I can do about it now, anyway."

She blinked and stared up at him, her eyes bloodshot but without that glazed look he'd seen earlier when the tequila and the tears flowed. "Fucking starving."

That brought a smile to his face. "I hear ya," he said through a sudden yawn, "but I don't think I can eat another fucking loaf of Italian bread or any more of those croutons. If we had some power, we'd be set."

"I had enough raw spinach to keep a girl regular for a year."

"At least the toilets are working."

"The whole restaurant is a toilet."

"Bonus!"

"Well, if we had some lights and electricity, you could whip us up something." Jessie smiled, but the smile turned into a wince, and she grabbed her head with both hands. "Good thing that bottle was half empty."

"Bet," said Haze. "We got all the fixins. But I dunno if I wanna go in that freezer; shit's still cold now, and I don't think my shirt's dry yet." He eyed the gray tee draped over one of the dish drying racks.

"But maybe we could grab some crab and take it with us. Doggy bag."

Jessie sat up, her body a little apart from Haze now, and he immediately missed the warmth of her. She leaned up against the wall next to him and pulled her feet up underneath her, pruny toes peeking out from under her knees. Her socks and boots were sitting close-by to dry out, which was probably a waste of time like his shirt. Nothing was gonna be dry any time soon.

"Shit, plenty outside already cooked, if that's how you wanna go." It had seemed like a good joke when it was coming down the pipe from his brain to his mouth, but as soon as it passed his lips, Haze couldn't help from frown. Yeah, they'd smoked a couple of crabs, but there were two friends down outside under the waves, too.

He swallowed, wiped his nose so as not to look like he was wiping his eyes. Jessie had cried enough for the both of them, hadn't she? Cried and poured. Now they just needed to move on, to get on down the road, as it were, and get somewhere safe. Maybe his place in Highlandtown, otherwise known as the Canton Annex, if you spoke *Yuppie*, was still standing. It was up the hill far enough it shouldn't be under water, he figured. He would take Jessie there, if they could just get out of the restaurant.

Haze yawned again, stretched. Now that Jessie was up, he could move a little, but it was slow going. His ass was asleep, and his legs, most notably his knee, were stiff and protested his decision to swing around to a sitting position. When he did, his Jordan's hit the water. They were already ruined, so what the fuck. It was his crotch that was the concern now anyway; wet underwear and wet jeans could tear some shit up after a while. "Damn. This is how I used to feel after a game. What I wouldn't give for the whirlpool again."

"Tough life. I'll take an extra strength Tylenol or six and I'll be alright."

"And a fresh pair of pants."

Jessie nodded.

"And then what?"

"And then I want to get the hell outta here and maybe go get some crab cakes." She half-smiled, but Haze grinned to let her know it was cool.

"And crab bisque. And crab fucking fritters." There was nothing else to do now - laugh and move on. Or be angry. Crying wasn't going to get them out of this mess or bring Damien back, and maybe they could down some crab later and feel like they were getting a little of their own revenge. Haze took a deep breath, feeling an energy surge, the muscles in his neck and jaw tensing up.

"And crab some-shit-no one's-ever-thought-of-yet. Crab biscuits. Crab and grits. Crabby toast. Crab sausage. Crab cereal even - Crabby O's." Jessie snatched the empty tequila bottle up and tossed it across the room. It thumped against the metal door of the freezer and kerplunked in the water below.

"We gonna eat those bitches til we puke." Haze smiled despite the headache that was threatening to tear him apart.

But Jessie just held her head in her hands, a pained look plastered on her face. "Stop it. I got the brain pain."

"Me, too, and we found everything here except power to cook with and some damn aspirin."

"Well, maybe it's time to get moving then and find our way the fuck out of here," she said and reached for her socks. "I'm really gonna need a pedi when this is over." She slipped them on and then pulled the first boot over her foot, then the second, and yanked on the laces.

"And some new boots, too. Damn, these were my favorites. Got them at DSW like three weeks ago."

"That's in Canton, right?"

"Yeah, by Target. That and Designer Shoe Warehouse. My two favorite places to shop."

Haze watched her, shaking his head, then stared past her to the two black bags that sat on the end of the counter, the whole reason he was sitting here with her in the first place. He could get her some new boots, a pedicure, and anything else she wanted. The bags made it true, or rather what was in them. Call them Benjamins, dead presidents, or greenbacks, there were a lot of them, and they were found money now, weren't they? There was no taking them back and saying, "Sorry". That was straight jail time there. And he didn't know who Damien's contact was. Shit was just done and over with now. All he had to do was walk out of the horror movie they'd been trapped in all day, and he'd have fifty large in hand. Seed money.

Money he'd yet to explain or even show Jessie. And what was he supposed to say? They'd downed half the tequila before he'd gone that far, and sitting there, watching her get herself together, he wished he had another bottle. He needed it - to tell the story of what happened before they'd met, how Damien had shot the money dude and he'd found himself trapped. It was the nightmare he'd always been afraid of, and now it had come round to get him, like the boogie man his old auntie had warned him about when he was growing up. Go to sleep or the boogie man will get you. Eat your peas or the boogie man will get you. Stay off the corner or the boogie man - maybe the cops - will get you. He'd never seen the boogie man, but he'd seen the cops. He didn't want to see either this time.

And he didn't want to see Jessie's reaction, but if this day was going to go any farther, she had to know. And then he'd have to deal with it, whatever happened.

"Fuck," came a voice from the kitchen door as it swung open. A silhouette in the shape of Jessie's ex appeared and stopped. "You in here?"

"Who?" Jessie looked up from her laces.

"You, and him."

"Haze. His name is Haze."

Haze smirked, knowing Rick couldn't see him. "What up?"

"Cooler Guy - his name is Josh. He and that idiot Cole are up on the roof throwing cocktails at everything."

"Like what? Pina coladas and margaritas and shit? Shaken not stirred?"

"Fuck off, dude. Firebombs. The same ones we were using earlier."

"Da fuck? Motherfuckers drunk?"

"Them? They've been drinking all afternoon. I don't think there's a beer left in the place. Or any Fireball. Now they're working through the rail vodka and rum."

"Wait," said Jessie, "all afternoon? What time is it?"

"It's like eight, I think." He looked at his watch, tapped on it. "This might be right."

Haze straightened up. "Eight at night?" No way, he thought. It couldn't be eight o'clock, could it? How long had they been asleep? "What the fuck you been doing all this time?"

"I was asleep while you were in here doing whatever," Rick growled "I don't wanna hear about it. I was fucking exhausted. Now those dumb fucks are up there setting everything on fire, and those crabs are everywhere."

Haze sighed and slid off the counter into the water. This shit was never going to end...unless maybe he could grab Jessie and they could sneak out the back, leaving the rest of the jokers behind. But he was only two steps toward Rick before he realized he couldn't do that. The runners he couldn't leave behind - they were cool, and they'd saved his life, after all. And Rick? As shitty as he'd been to Jessie, and the way he'd clung to that girl Roxie right in front of her, maybe he didn't deserve any respect, but he couldn't leave that guy either. It just wasn't in him.

And the money? Haze stopped halfway to the kitchen door, watching Rick turn his back and walk away, then turned to Jessie, who was slipping down into the water, as well, and pulling her backpack on. His eyes shifted to the bags, then back to Jessie, and he shook his head. It wasn't time just yet. He had some other bullshit to take care of first. "Leave the bag, Jessie. We'll go sort those two fools out and come back down, k? We need to get the fuck out of here; if it's really eight, I'm late."

"For what?"

"I don't know, but I'm not staying here in this shit any longer. I want this to be over and go find somewhere else to be. Wanna go with?"

Jessie smiled as she walked by and said, "Yeah," as she slid her fingers across his chin.

"Bet."

They hadn't taken two steps though before a massive boom shook the old boat-shaped restaurant and the wall to their right buckled. Haze froze, ready to grab Jessie and run, but the inside hull of the fake ocean liner held.

"Fuck!" said Rick, spinning away. "They're burning everything. Gonna kill us all."

But the words hadn't even left his lips before screams echoed in the dining room. Rick threw open the door, and Haze pushed up behind him, holding Jessie back. In the semi-darkness, he could make out some bodies - a few hitting the water at the bottom of the steps and couple crossing the room opposite the bar, where a bunch of tables had been shoved together to form a makeshift platform. The runners came from the right; the stairs puked out Muscles and Ashley.

"Run!" she screamed. "He's on fire!"

"What the ...?"

But Haze couldn't even finish his sentence before he saw a bright light flicker in the hollow of the dark staircase, and he yanked Rick back and out of the way to make room for the others just as Cooler Guy appeared, looking all Johnny Storm from the Fantastic Four - flame on! - and screaming like a banshee. The real-life Human Torch stumbled down the last few steps and hit the water with a sickening sploosh, but instead of the flames fizzling out in the face of their natural enemy, the water erupted into flame and the fire streaked across the top of the black liquid in every direction - heading right for them.

"Run!" yelled Haze, and he skipped out of the way as Muscles powered through. Then he slammed the door as fast as he could in the waist deep cold and stepped back, waiting for the flames to flash through the gaps in the swinging doors and swallow him up next. He turned to look for Jessie one more time, and she was right there, moving in with her fire extinguisher. She aimed the cone and fired just as they all heard the crackle and hiss of the flames, saw a tongue of light flick through the gaps.

"Stand back," she shouted and squeezed the trigger again.

"We're outta here," said Haze, shouting over the icy blast of the CO_2. "Now. Rick, Muscles - sorry, Cole, get that back door open, grab whatever you can find as a weapon."

"The park?"

"Go!"

There was no more argument and no more waiting. He turned back to watch Jessie hit the door with little spurts of the extinguisher's mixture, then reached over and snatched the red and silver contraption out of her hands. She protested, but his words silenced her.

"Get back to the table and empty both of those black bags into your backpack. Don't ask questions. Please."

Her mouth opened then closed, and she was gone, while Haze backed slowly away from the door. Each time a flicker of flame peeked through the split doors, he blasted it with a little of the cold stuff, but it wasn't going to last. The extinguisher was already light when he took it from Jessie. And it felt lighter with each trigger squeeze.

Haze chanced a glance back, saw Jessie busy with her task. He couldn't see the look on her face or read her expression in the dark, but he knew what was coming. And it didn't matter what questions she would have; she wasn't asking them now. She understood that they had no time to talk. Meanwhile, just past her he could see four figures fucking with the back door and seemingly making no progress.

"Break it the fuck down, Muscles, you pussy!"

Haze was surprised by his own words and suddenly missed Damien. He fired another shot of the cold stuff at the door and wished it was his friend trying to get through; it would have been a funny prank. But instead, there was a wall of flame looking for something to eat, and they were next on the menu.

18

JESSIE TRIED NOT TO stare at the wads of rolled up tens and twenties she was moving from one bag to the other. How much fucking money was in there? Ten thousand? Fifty? A hundred? She'd never seen anything like it - well, movies didn't count, did they? She'd seen plenty of movies with gangsters or hoods making off with a heist, or sexy George Clooney-like wise guys ripping off some big-named bankrollers. There'd even been those awesome movies with the crew of fast-driving crooks you had to love. And every one of them had been a criminal you wanted to roll with, to ride off into the sunset with. Too boss; too bitchin'. They were itching for a better piece of life, something she'd always wanted, too, but at what cost?

Rick had always had his schemes, but he was small-time. Taco Tuesdays or some shit. They should start up a Grand Marnier club and try to develop an exclusive clientele. Or his suggestion that they try and be more like Woody's Island Bar and do a Caribbean thing - maybe Jessie and some other female staff would wear bikinis and he'd do some board shorts and flip flops.

"If you want me in a thong, you gotta sport a banana hammock," she'd said after that suggestion, and he'd offered to go out and get one right away.

She smiled as she stuffed the last roll of cold hard and slightly damp cash into her backpack. She tugged on the zipper and felt the resistance; it was maxed out but closing. She was about to walk out of there looking like they'd just robbed a limo full of strippers.

A thump behind her spun her around, and she saw Muscles rear back and hit the door again, pummeling it with his shoulder. One moment he was there, and the next he was gone, through the door and splashing down with a mouthful of curses.

"We're going!" shouted Rick, and the other shapes pushed through the door like rats from a sinking ship.

"Haze," said Jessie, turning back to get his attention, but he was already there, his hand cupping her elbow and propelling her forward and out into the inky blackness beyond. Then he released her, and she could feel as much as see him turn and shut the door behind him.

"Shit's getting old," he said, his back to the door.

"Watch out. My foot," came a voice in her left ear, and Jessie spun, her arm coming up to block whatever was there, only to find the girl in Muscle's shirt, whatever her name was, standing there. She was inches away and Jessie could barely see her.

"Sorry. I can't see."

"Nobody can," said Rick, a shadow among shadows in front of her. "Lights out all over the city. No stars. No moon."

"How the fuck are we going anywhere then?" It was Muscles this time. His voice was distinctive and unexpectedly laced with fear. Some grumbles around them indicated a similar sentiment.

"Grab my hand," said Jessie to Ashley and she reached out, her fingers searching until she felt the other girl latch on. "Everyone, grab a hand. We'll go like this so we don't get separated."

"But the crabs?"

There was no answer from anyone on that question. Everyone knew the answers anyway, didn't they? The city was blindingly dark. Their one safe place to hide was gone. There were still giant crabs out there somewhere. And they had no weapons at all. Hell, Ashley didn't even have pants or shoes. And they were going to try and walk half a mile through whatever other landmines were lurking out there between them and the park?

Jessie shrugged. It wasn't unlike the end of a good bar crawl. Only usually no one died during a bar crawl.

"Let's go," she said. She felt Haze's fingers intertwine with hers, felt the tug forward, and she pulled on Ashley's hand and moved out. "Everyone link up. We're getting to the park now or we're going home in body bags."

"Whoa," said Haze as he led the way up the back alley. "That's some fucking motivation right there." He chuckled and squeezed her hand.

"Well, I gotta get us outta here; I've got some cash to spend, don't you know? Baby needs new boots."

She felt his fingers squeeze her hand again, and then they slowed up as they came to the end of the alley and Boston Street opened in front of them. What they saw there was nothing more than a ghost town with a sort of haunted glow about it. Somewhere across the street, behind a series of crumbled rowhomes that once sported businesses, a few bars and one of the oldest diners in America - Jessie could remember a few greasy breakfasts there - a fire raged, throwing its eerie light up into the heavy clouds that still dominated the Baltimore sky. She stared at the sky, watched the flames reflected there as if it was lightning playing across the bottom of an incoming storm.

She shivered. It was like every disaster movie she'd ever seen, all of it sitting right in front of her as if she were wearing those 3D glasses that were so popular. Only this monster movie was very real. She could feel the cold of the water numbing her legs, the subtle shift as invisible waves swept in from the harbor. She inhaled the stink of it, that trashy, near-death reek that settled over the waterfront neighborhoods after a heavy rain, a constant reminder that the time when the harbor was swimmable was long past. And somewhere out there, on the right out of sight, the faint warbling of crabs drifted across the quiet darkness.

Five or six more blocks, she told herself. That's as far as they needed to get, and they'd be safe. At least she hoped so. And then what? She shook her head. There was little point to speculating. They had to get through this last bit first.

Haze scanned the street left, then right, Jessie following his eyes, trying to see through the gloom. Boston Street was as dead as the rest of the city, a dark, watery graveyard, the cars lining the street little more than tombstones poking out above the inky flood, marking the final resting places of a few rusted-out Fords or the occasional high end Yuppie wagon. There were no lights in any windows, no engines running, no screams - only the quiet breathing of six exhausted and scared people tucked into the faux safety of a Baltimore alley.

"Right now would be a great time for the National Guard to show up," said Haze. "Where the fuck's the Army when you need them?"

"They always show up too late in the movies," said Jessie. "So, we best not wait."

"Yeah, but now what?" said Haze, and the wall behind them exploded.

Suddenly blind, ears ringing, Jessie felt herself lifted into the air and slammed against something unyielding, and then she was down, under the water, silent screams streaming out of her open mouth in tiny bubbles. She thrashed, trying to right herself, unsure of which way was up, eyes open but seeing nothing, and then something hit her and settled in on her like a giant sitting down on a mountain top throne. She screamed again, trying to hold in a little air, hands seeking some kind of purchase, feet kicking out to get her some momentum, some way to get out from under whatever crushed her body into the hard concrete, but it was useless. She grunted out a few futile bubbles, feeling her lungs burning, the blackness closing in past her eyes, and then she knew it was over.

A last stretch of sheer panic wracked the dim light that shown inside her mind as she felt that fateful claw engulf her body, and she blurted out an unheard, Old Bay-laced curse before she was ripped out of the water and sputtered out a final scream.

"I got you, Jessie!" Haze's voice played through the fog in her mind, a cruel joke from hours before, when he'd risked his life and plummeted over the edge of the wall at Woody's to save her from a fall. What a cruel joke, she thought, feeling the crush in her ribs, the pain shooting through her legs as the monster began to snap her in half.

"I got you," came the voice again. "It's okay. Breathe. Breathe, goddamn it. Come on. We gotta move. Now. Jessie. Let's go. Let's go."

The words swam over her like waves, far away as if they were in a dream. They wanted her back, and all she had to do was click her heels together three times and say... "There's no place like home," she sputtered and opened her eyes.

Haze stared back at her, his face smeared with blood, his nose bent awkwardly to the side. "Come on, baby, we're not in Kansas anymore. We gots to go now. Come on."

Jessie blinked, eyes unfocused then focusing again, pain shooting into her chest with every unexpected breath. "What?" was all she could muster. She squinted past Haze at the bright flames and what was left of the old boat-shaped restaurant. And beyond that, she saw the shapes in the water again. "Crabs!"

"We're out!" hollered Haze, and he swung her around, ignoring her groan.

Jessie stumbled forward, only the waist-deep water keeping her from falling flat on her face. "Help me," she cried, but Haze was still right there, arm around her in that crushing bear hug that made her wince again.

"I got you, baby. Let's fucking move."

"I can't walk," she said, gritting her teeth as they squeezed between two parked cars.

"I don't care if one of your fucking legs falls off," barked Haze in her ear. "You fucking move your ass now!"

Jessie turned, saw the fire in his eyes, the blood dripping down from the cut on his forehead, and gritted her teeth, feeling everything coming to a boil. All this bullshit, she thought. Climbing, running, ducking, hiding from a bunch of fucking crabs that oughta be someone's lunch. All she wanted to do was turn and shoot, throw something, just let it all hang out with a rocket launcher or smart bomb or something she'd be armed with in one of their Xbox games. But they didn't have shit, except harsh words and some spit. And she was all outta spit.

"The others?" The thought hit her and she would have stopped and turned around if Haze hadn't had her all wrapped up.

"They're coming," he said, grunting as they stepped up onto the sidewalk farther down Boston Creek, formerly Boston Street.

Jessie chanced a glance back and saw them, black silhouettes in front of the building they'd left in flames - four shapes, each of them moving slowly, but each of them moving. And just beyond them, the oval shells of the creatures that would revolutionize crab cakes - with that much meat, who needed filler? If only she had a flame thrower...

Off they went, like a chain of paper cut-out dolls, squeezing through a pair of half-submerged, formerly parallel parked cars. Haze pulled her forward like a locomotive that thinks it can, powering through the waist-deep blackness, hugging the walls of a large building on the right, then whipping around the corner in front of a liquor store without hesitation. Jessie was pleased to see they weren't going to stop again; they'd had enough alcohol-related incidents for one day, she thought, although that went against the rules of the neighborhood - and Haze kept them moving forward, up Fleet Street, then left again.

All the while, the water was dropping away. From her waist at Captain James, it was down to Jessie's knees once they hit Eastern Avenue and turned right. Ahead she knew Patterson Park waited. Only a block to go and then they would be home free, or at least that's what they thought. Half the day they'd had no real destination at all, except to get out of the water and away from the crabs. If that had meant heading down Martin Luther King and into some West Side neighborhoods from Baltimore's famous television show, The Wire, she would have been fine with that. All she'd wanted - all they'd wanted was to get someplace safe and dry, and it looked like the bit about being dry was about to happen. The question that remained was if it was going to be safe.

And then the water was gone, and it was all dry land in front of them. Jessie almost cheered, suddenly mobile like they hadn't been all day, only it was then that she really felt the searing pain in her left foot and knew she wasn't going to get much farther without the man who was acting as her crutch. He was limping, too, she noticed, and grunting with each step, but she couldn't see enough of him to know what was wrong, only hear the hiss of his breath from between his teeth.

A moment later they were at the intersection of Eastern and Patterson Park, and Rick was calling from behind to go left. Haze hesitated, bending over, hands on knees, letting Jessie lean against the telephone pole there for support. His breath was coming in rasps and wheezes, and his voice was quiet, like a gasp. "How much more? Where to?"

"Another two blocks, Haze. You can do it." She swallowed, looked down the darkened street toward what she knew awaited them. "We can do it."

From out of the shadows, two figures appeared, Muscles and Ashley, then two more, the runners. Rick was close behind, leaving them all gasping at the corner like a crew of novice marathoners in October. Jessie's feet certainly felt like she'd run too many miles in sneakers that didn't fit right. The boots, she knew, were trashed, and the socks were, too. And underneath it all, there would be blisters that she didn't even want to think about. Every step was agony, every breath an exercise in perseverance. And she could see the same all around her; there was no telling what Ashley's feet looked like - every girl in Baltimore knew you couldn't walk home from a night out in heels, but to walk home barefoot was maybe a fate worse than death.

Then she heard it, and she knew they all heard it, too, when collectively they all stopped breathing - that creepy warbling, that haunting sound that spiked up the matted down blonde hairs on her forearms.

"They're coming," said Rick. "And there are a shit ton of them."

"Fuck that, dude," said Muscles. "I can't keep going like this. I can't see and I think I dislocated my shoulder when that bomb went off. Ain't there another plan that doesn't involve more running?"

"Better move your ass, Cole," said Ashley. "You can't fuck me if you're dead."

That seemed to clear the air, and suddenly Muscles was standing tall. "What's our next stop, boss?"

Jessie chuckled. Motivation was the key to most things. She couldn't see the big guy that well, but she understood. She'd seen his motivation, and if helping a pretty girl to survive a natural disaster that included killer crabs got him laid, well, it was hard to argue with that. Especially since her potential suitors were quickly dwindling down to zero. Rick - well, there was no telling how he felt right now. And the runners - she was pretty sure they were together. Nothing wrong with that, she thought; gay men were some of her best customers. And they tipped great.

"The pagoda. We're going to the pagoda," said Rick, pointing up the street. "It's about two blocks away. We'll be safe there."

"Safe for how long?" said Ashley. "Those crabs aren't exactly going to wander off because they're missing their favorite shows and they forgot to DVR them."

"And where are the cops?" said Mike, chiming in.

"And where is everyone else?" said Marty. "Was there an evacuation while we were resting and firebombing ourselves?" The last part of the sentence came out as more of a raspy growl than anything.

"Move, everyone. Go," said Rick.

And he was right, Jessie decided, because suddenly everything went quiet, as if they were collectively holding their breath in response to Rick's warning. Then out of the darkness they heard the click-clack of little feet, or paws, or whatever the ends of crab legs were called. Jessie decided she didn't care enough to find out. She was ready to go, even though she just wanted to fall in the street right there and take a nap.

Where was a cab when a girl needed one, for Christ's sake? Or at least an Uber.

Then, before they could take a step into the street, Jessie heard a siren and saw flashing lights, and a white ambulance bounced out of the darkness on Eastern Ave, coming right at them as if to make the corner. It skidded, tires shrieking, and tipped over, slamming down on its side with a metallic crunch and slid across the pavement until it took out the telephone pole Jessie and friends had been huddling under and crashed into the former corner branch of Eastern Bank.

19

HAZE PULLED HIMSELF up into a sitting position, trying to breathe through the pain in his leg all while trying not to breathe at all because of the pain in his chest. Beside him, Jessie was on her hands and knees, caught up in a fit of coughing, her eyes flashing with anger while she tried to catch her breath. The rest of their crew was scattered nearby, all of them down on the ground. Groans filled the air, taking the place of the shrieking siren, and each of them pushed to their feet like zombies coming back to life for the first time, herky jerky first steps and all.

He was done. Angry, tired, hurt, and tired of being angry and hurt. And tired of crabs and the stupid shit that kept happening. He was tired of it all - of the dark, of the way the lights on the ambulance flashed, the sound of bits and pieces of the crumbling building falling onto the metal hood of the overturned truck. He was tired of how his pants crunched around his crotch and how his socks squished between his toes. Tired of how he couldn't breathe through his nose at all and how his right ear stung. Tired of the blood that kept getting in his eyes and how his favorite t-shirt was torn and ruined. And mostly he was tired of wondering when the next complete bullshit thing was going to happen and take them all out. Hadn't they had enough yet?

They'd gotten away from the cops, fallen into the middle of an earthquake, been nearly drowned and crushed and eaten, been chased by giant crustaceans, almost been arrested or shot by the cops, almost burned to death, then almost killed in an explosion. Then almost run over by a rescue vehicle. Haze was sure he was forgetting something, but he'd remember it later in time for the memoir. *Crabquake*, he'd call it. Sounded a little dumb, but it worked, and he smiled a little to himself as he stood there in the middle of the street, staring like a dummy at the flipped ambulance and shaking his head. But for now, they had to jet. But check the ambulance first. Maybe there was someone there who needed help. Maybe there was someone who could offer some.

It turned out that the back of the truck was empty, one of the doors hanging open by only one of the hinges; the other was gone. The cab held nothing more than a single dead man who looked less like an ambulance driver or EMT and more like a bum with every second. No help there. Haze stood beside the back of the truck while Jessie rummaged through the debris, then when she popped out with a handful of bandages and a flashlight, they moved out.

It was a long walk up the street - up because everything here was uphill now, and Haze felt every step of it. They'd crossed the street to keep the jumble of parked cars between them and the pursuing monsters, the flashlight playing out over the wet cement. It was a simple comfort, the idea that they finally had some kind of light, even if daylight was probably the only light anyone was interested in seeing. Every few yards they stopped, each of them gasping for breath, claiming inability to continue, and grumbling, but the moment they heard the clickety clack of the crab legs and that soft warbling in the distance, they pushed on.

"They're like fucking bloodhounds, these things," mumbled Marty on one of their short breaks.

"Maybe we can catch one and sell it to a circus," offered Muscles.

"More likely you'll be the one in the circus," somebody replied - Haze couldn't see who it was, and he didn't recognize the voice since it was half-drowned in his own coughing. For a second, he thought it was D, his boy; it was just the kind of thing he'd say. But no....

A few minutes later, the pagoda came into view, or what was left of it. Not exactly what Haze had been expecting, he nevertheless recognized it for what it was the moment they got close. About three stories tall, it towered over everything except the tallest trees - or it once was; now it was a dark heap at the top of the hill.

"No!" said Rick, and he lurched ahead.

But at the top of the hill, when they finally caught up, they found him sitting next to the wreckage of the old metal structure. Haze plopped down next to him, his legs nearly done, his ankle screaming. This wasn't part of the plan, he thought, but what was today?

"Now what?" he said, the words pushing past his lips with every effort he could muster. This was pretty much the end of the line, one way or another. It was hard to deny it. He'd seen how the rest of them were getting along, how they dropped to the grass and put their heads down. They were done. "We staying here? This place isn't safe."

"And where the hell is everyone?" chimed in Jessie. "The cops? The National Guard? We haven't seen a single person anywhere. I wish we had a radio or something."

"Who knows?" Rick shrugged. "It's up to us still. And now we have to make it through the rest of the night somehow. Do we stay here? Do we keep running?"

"I don't know about you," said Jessie, "but I'm done. I just..."

"I know." Haze settled in on the grass and leaned back on some piece of metal that had once been part of the pagoda. For once it was nice to sit somewhere that wasn't soaking wet, although the steady drizzle made everything damp.

"Admittedly I was hoping this place would still be standing, and we could stay here," said Rick, the exhaustion in his voice just as plain. "I was volunteering last weekend to set up the cannons here for the bicentennial of the War of 1812 next weekend. Everything was set."

"I think that's gonna have to be postponed, don't you think?" Jessie chuckled, then coughed.

"Yeah, but the fireworks don't," said Rick, and Haze could see his grin in the glow of the flashlight. "The cannons work, and we have projectiles and powder for them. The plan was to put three of the cannons on swivel mounts so they could be tilted back and fireworks fired out of them with these plastic projectiles we made just for the occasion. They'd fly up, arcing into the air like cannonballs from the ships bombarding Fort McHenry and explode like any other fireworks over the harbor. It was gonna be fucking cool."

"And now?" Haze was getting a little impatient, a little too tired of Rick and his ideas. All he needed now was a safe place to sit, to lay his head, and maybe a tank. Where was a tank when you needed one?

"Now we're going to do what the troops in Baltimore did two hundred years ago - we're going to defend this hill. All night if we have to."

Haze looked at Jessie, and they both looked at Rick. He must have been hit in the head with a brick or two-by-four back at Captain James. He was talking gibberish now. No way they could sit there and fire cannons at the crabs all night. And with what? Fireworks? Were they supposed to dazzle the damned things to death. A few 'oooh' and 'ahhh' moments weren't going to get the job done, based on what he'd seen all day of those things. Haze took a deep breath to keep himself from telling Rick exactly what he could do with his projectiles and let his eyes wander over the shapes that sat around them, all of them surely listening and none of them saying a thing.

He wondered if they could see the expression on his face. Jessie had turned off the flashlight when they sat down on the cracked concrete just behind a pair of cannons that waited, innocent now but maybe ready to do some damage if they had just had some cannonballs. What a waste! All this way, he thought, all the way out of the shithole they'd half-walked half-swam out of for nothing.

"Oh," said Rick suddenly, as if his brain was running a little behind, "and we've got more than fireworks. We've got this." And he produced a large, wet plastic bag with the words Carry Out on the side, and he dumped out more than a dozen little red and yellow boxes marked with the words Old Bay. He grinned like a schoolboy. "Told you what we were looking for at Captain James - something like pepper spray. This'll do just fine."

Haze swallowed, not yet ready to believe anything that had happened since he woke up that morning. It was all too surreal, and he was sure just then that he'd wake up in his bed alone in his little basement studio in Highlandtown. He had the late shift at the restaurant, and there'd be college football on TV, for sure. Bama was playing, and he'd be cleaning up, probably washing some dishes with Herbie, and watching the game in the kitchen.

Now, they were about to load some cannons with fireworks and Old Bay and defend an old battlefield from a new foe?

"You're fucking with me, bro. I ain't got time for that." Haze shook his head and closed his eyes. Then they heard it - that noise that Haze knew would haunt his dreams for years to come, and his eyes popped open. The warbling. They were still coming.

"We need the projectiles from the storage shed. The wicks, the long matches, the powder. It's all in there."

"Where?"

"Just come with me," said Rick, "and we'll get everything and bring it back, load these cannons and start blasting, but we don't have time to discuss this, Haze. You in?"

Haze just stared back at him, knowing the answer already. He was suited up, helmet on, and the play had been called. It was game time again. Only enough time for a Hail Mary. "Fuck it. Let's go."

It was easier said than done - standing, then running, following Rick, the flashlight's beam waving wildly as they bolted around the wreckage of the fallen pagoda. His ankle screamed, like his knee had before, but he ran anyway. There was no back-up quarterback and there were no more time outs. This was it: sudden death.

They reached the storage shed in what seemed like an eternity, knowing that there were five people left behind, five people that were completely vulnerable and in the pitch black while those things were coming. Haze snatched the flashlight and shined its beam on the combination lock while Rick worked the numbers. His fingers flew, but he had to stop himself and calm down after two failed attempts. Then on the third try they were in, sliding the doors apart and pushing past some decorated trash cans that smelled of new paint to the back of the shed, where the shells were piled on pallets.

"How the fuck do we get all of this shit down to the pagoda?" Haze stared at the black plastic casings on one side and what had to be the powder pellets on the other.

"Trash can. Dump it all in a trash can," said Rick, and Haze went right to work, throwing it all in there haphazardly while Rick searched around for the fuses and long matches. A little yelp of triumph announced their location, and then they were hoisting up the fifty-gallon drum full of explosives and pushing back through the other trash cans and into the night.

If Haze had thought it was slow going before, it was even slower now. Agonizingly slow as his limp became more pronounced, and he felt fingers of fiery pain shooting up his leg. The clock was ticking, he knew, so he just dealt with it, gritting his teeth against the pain, his breath hissing from between his clenched lips. Game time - just like that last drive against City High when he'd marched them eighty-two yards in a minute forty-two seconds for the game tying touchdown and a two-point conversion for the win. He'd done it all on one leg, his knee threatening to buckle with every snap of the ball, every dropback, every scramble for yardage that they'd absolutely needed because the coverage was too good. Sixty-three of those yards were all on Haze's shoulders, and afterward he'd learned that his MCL was partially torn, and his season was over.

That time, he realized, could come again tonight, but not until he'd played out the rest of the game. It would just have to wait.

Moments later, they spilled the can out onto the grass between the two cannons, and Rick and Jessie went to work performing a little surgery on each projectile. She'd popped open each of the cans of Old Bay while they were gone, and Rick twisted open each mini cannonball, seventeen in all, so she could pour in a handful of the spice Baltimoreans swore was the key to doing anything with crabs - even fighting with them. After this, Haze knew that red and yellow logo would be world famous.

"Here they come," shouted Muscles, and he pulled Ashley back toward the wreckage of the pagoda, the others following close behind.

"Load 'em up," said Haze, trying to keep his voice down.

"This is what you do," said Rick, demonstrating, "put in the charge pellet, then projectile, then slide the wick down through the hole in the top, aim and light." He scrambled over to the cannon on the left, bringing some of the supplies with him. "Jessie, you help keep us supplied, but be careful. The cannons get hot after a couple of shots."

"Gotcha," she said, still kneeling on the ground, screwing the tops back on a few of the shells.

"And remember this, we only have seventeen of these things, so make your shots count."

A moment later the first crab-shaped silhouette moved into view, something blacker than the night waddling forward and warbling. "Tallyho," shouted Rick, and he swung his cannon around, struck his match and stepped back.

The spark on the wick sputtered, then flared, burning quickly down to the metal, and then the cannon roared, throwing up a massive cloud of greenish mist like a halo around the end of the gun. Whatever blasted out was too fast for Haze to track, but when it hit, there was no doubting what they'd fired. The Fourth of July erupted in the face of the nearest crab only a dozen or so yards away, basking the hill in the fury of a dozen different firework explosions.

All of it was shrouded in a reddish tint, which had to be the Old Bay. Behind him, he heard the most amazing thing he thought he could even hear: a cheer. It erupted from Jessie's lips next to him, and before he knew it, he was hollering, too, watching the fireworks pop off one after the other, and then the world went dark again, leaving him blinking and seeing after-flashes every time he closed his eyes. It was intense! It was like their overtime touchdown, only the first score wasn't over, and he wasn't even sure it worked.

What'd he seen was a field lit up, revealing dozens of opposing players, more crabs than they'd seen all day, and more than he could count in the sudden flash of light, but what he'd never heard on the field of play was plain in the still of the night: the unnatural scream of a crab. It echoed across the grassy field like a wolf's howl or a siren - he wasn't sure which. But he did know that they'd scored a direct hit. The question was if it'd had any real effect, or was it just pissing that crab off?

"There!" shouted Jessie.

Another crab was almost on them, but Haze was ready, the wick already in place. He swiveled the cannon around - it was harder than he'd thought it would be - and aimed while Jessie struck the match and touched it to the wick. Then he stood back and watched the fuse burn down, his heart hammering inside his chest, a sudden rush of adrenaline pushing the pain back from his leg until it was just a dull throb. Then the cannon erupted, and the shot fired out, nailing the massive crustacean full in whatever face it could claim to have and exploding into a dozen reddish-gold showers.

Just as Haze raised up his hands in the international sign for touchdown, Rick was firing off another round, and Jessie was back, shell and powder pellet in hand for the reload. "Keep moving, baby," she said. "We're going to win this motherfucker."

Haze smiled just as a star-spangled spectacular lit up the grass a few dozen yards away, and then he was reloaded and swinging his cannon around, target already in sight. "Fire in the hole," he yelled out and touched the wick with the new match. A few seconds later, another crab was enveloped in a red, white and blue celebration, the popping fireworks echoing across the field.

Then suddenly, there was a new light display, a spotlight playing down from the heavens and across the field just as Rick fired again. Haze turned, his ears picking up the whoop-whoop of a helicopter as it came in from behind them, a voice booming down from above like an avenging angel. "Hold your fire and fall back. We have troops inbound." Those were the only words before the spotlight settled on the nearest crab and a roar like a giant fart ripped the night in two as the helicopter opened up with an automatic weapon, ripping into the massive shell. In seconds the crab was down on the ground, its body shredded, and the light was playing across the field to find a new target.

Haze jumped as that roar filled the air again, felt Jessie pulling on his arm. "We're done now," she shouted over the gunfire. "We did it, baby." Her fingers gripped and pulled while her lips pressed into his neck, then his cheek, then against his lips as she spun him around. He let her guide him, first with her mouth, then with her hands as they backed away from the battlefield, and before they'd taken more than a dozen shaky steps, he could see the lights bouncing across the field below them, see the outlines of the Humvees.

The cavalry had finally come.

20

JESSIE SMILED FROM across the table, knowing she looked just as shitty as Haze did. He sipped a Coke from a can, each move slow, deliberate as if he was still feeling the pain. But she knew he was hopped up on the same drugs she was, feeling no pain. His nose was bandaged, his right ear, too, and his forehead had a dozen stitches in it underneath a swatch of white tape. He looked like he'd been in a gang fight or an all-day battle with a pack of giant killer crabs.

She giggled and swallowed a mouthful of water, wondering when the television crews would arrive or Geraldo Rivera would show up. They had a story to tell that would keep them on the talk show circuit for months, didn't they? And then a tell-all book, ghost-written, of course - how would they have time to write themselves when they were busy being on TV everywhere and consulting on the graphic novel that would no doubt feature them? And who would play her in the shitty straight-to-video movie on the SyFy Channel? Not Tara Reid.

But what did it matter? What mattered was that it was over. The cavalry - in fact, the National Guard - had arrived just in time, like they were supposed to do, and they'd wiped the floor with the crabs. Those shells were no match for machine guns, rockets and grenades. Meanwhile, they'd been whisked into Humvees and rushed out of there, back to the "safe zone" in Greektown and at least half a mile from the flooded waterfront. What she'd learned there about the condition of downtown, the submergence of the Inner Harbor and most of Canton, the number of crabs infesting the city, and how more National Guard units were being called in to take on street sweeping duties was something she hadn't been prepared to believe. But they assured her it was true. The face of the Charm City would never be the same again.

She'd said goodbye to Rick then, watched them take him off to get cleaned up, his eyes searching hers for something that wasn't there anymore. He had her number, but there wasn't much point in using it, and she'd let him know as much in the few words they shared. Muscles and Ashley were gone, too, with their small crew, and the runners, who came out surprisingly unscathed, had been sent on to a temporary shelter for observation and safety. Only she and Haze had gotten really banged up, and for that they were sitting in a tent on the Johns Hopkins Bayview campus, which was still mostly intact despite the 7.1 on the Richter Scale that had shaken a lot of Baltimore to the ground the morning before.

Jessie sat cross-legged on her cot in a set of powder blue hospital scrubs and stared at Haze, saying nothing. Her eyes made all the words she needed for the moment. All except for the few she'd been saving, words that he knew were coming, and she could see the recognition on his face when she glanced over at the gray backpack next to her.

"Tell me about the money, Haze."

"It belonged to Damien," he said, not missing a beat. "Seed money, he called it. Where or who he was bringing it to, I don't wanna know, to tell you the truth, but it's ours now, and I think we should take it and go away, go far away."

"Like where?"

He sounded sincere enough, and truth be told, she didn't fucking care anymore, not after everything that had happened. She'd earned it; they'd earned it - whatever it was; however much it was. Hadn't they? Her whole life was turned upside down, and his? Well, she didn't know much about it, but maybe they could just start over, both of them.

"Costa Rica? Puerto Rico?" He shrugged, sipped at his Coke, shifted in his chair. "I just pulled that outta my ass. I had no game plan this morning, and I still got no game plan."

"Aruba?"

"Works for me. Don't got no passport...yet."

Jessie leaned over on the backpack like it was a pillow. "Just nowhere they have crabs, okay?"

"Bet," he said and raised his Coke can up in a token salute. "I'll put my two weeks' notice in tomorrow."

"Fuck 'em," said Jessie. "You're mine now. Just pack a bag, and we're outta here. I got my bag," she said, patting the backpack. "You feel me?"

Haze grinned back at her, a little pain behind it when he moved, but a whole lot of happy shining through his eyes. "Oh, you know it, girl. Now, let's creep the fuck up outta here. We got some shit to do."

The End

About the Author

A teacher by day, SJ Stone plies his wares at night on his laptop, where he's cranking out silly blog posts, socio-political commentary, poetry, short stories and novels at an excessive rate. If he was driving, he'd have been pulled over by now. Meanwhile, he has multiple novel projects in the works, all in various stages of development: some mostly done and some still in the idea stage, some nothing more than a thought.

SJ Stone lives in Baltimore with his wife, two yorkies and a weiner dog named Sloppy Joe. He's been around the world 13 times with the Navy, has jumped out of a plane three times, has two grown kids and has this idea that later in life he'll live in Aruba, kite surf all day and write bad novels all night.

Read more at https://www.sjstoneauthor.com/.